Refugee camp near Salzburg, Austria, ca. 1950.

DISCOVERING AMERICA

HELMUT FISCHER

authorHOUSE®

AuthorHouse™
1663 Liberty Drive
Bloomington, IN 47403
www.authorhouse.com
Phone: 1 (800) 839-8640

Published by AuthorHouse 07/11/2019

ISBN: 978-1-7283-1685-7 (sc)
ISBN: 978-1-7283-1684-0 (hc)
ISBN: 978-1-7283-1686-4 (e)

Library of Congress Control Number: 2019908534

Print information available on the last page.

CONTENTS

To my father

CHAPTER 1

GOD'S CHILDREN

From the rectory library, I could see the chestnut trees in the clouded square. Through the library's open door, I saw Monsignor Andreas Bruck and Father framed below the wooden cross on the wall behind Bruck's desk. The priest made a steeple of his hands. Against his black cassock, as he explained about America, his hands looked pale.

"It's a country of great promise."

Father seemed to wait for his "but."

"Of course, the moral dangers are immense."

Father shrugged politely. "I'm afraid no more than anywhere, Monsignor Bruck. I don't see a choice for us."

"Of course you're right, Herr Kemper. The century's been a disaster, and it all emanated from here. But I'm speaking of temptations—each soul's personal temptations. Freedom's not the answer to every individual dilemma." Bruck paused. "How old is Konrad?"

"Twelve."

"Chicago, is it?"

"By way of Bremerhaven and New York."

"You'll want to look out for him."

Bruck's face looked cavernous, unlike the fleshy features of Simon Dachnagl, our instructor in weekly religion class. Somehow Bruck resembled the curate in our bygone Salzburg camp. Priests everywhere seemed interested in my spiritual welfare. Bruck looked from Father toward his window and the church on the tree-lined square. I wasn't sure I liked his tone. He seemed to know what I needed even before I got to America.

As I waited in the rectory library, I saw Father nod. Books surrounded me on its walls, books I'd no longer get to borrow, including the shelf of boys' adventure tales, especially those by Karl May. On the low table before me lay copies of *Gotteskinder,* the monthly tract that Simon Dachnagl would hand out in religion hour. The latest cover of *God's Children* showed nuns feeding thin children in Africa.

"Political exhaustion, moral, it comes down to the same thing," Father said. On his courtesy call to Bruck, he wasn't about not to question things. I liked that. "We'll certainly keep in mind your admonition, Monsignor Bruck."

As the spiritual head of the parish, Andreas Bruck expressed regret and gratitude. "It's good of you to stop by, Herr Kemper. I've not been able to see many of the refugees off. But your family's been an asset to the parish, and Konrad's a fine student. We hate to see you go. So many dream of America."

I doubted Bruck knew about everything. Behind the scenes, maybe Dachnagl had curried his favor by painting me as a choirboy. His special charge was refugees.

"I'm afraid American public schools may have slipped beyond redemption," added Bruck. "They acquiesce to popular culture. It's regrettable. They're not like our grammar schools, plain but effective. They're not quite out of the old Wild West but lawless in their way."

Bruck paused strategically. "Have you considered parish schools?"

Father didn't know about them.

"Private schools run by the church. They teach the basics, and they offer Catholic values."

In the anteroom of the library, his words caused me to mull things over. The Wild West—it sounded promising. I'd learn about America. I wasn't so sure about the private schools. Just then, the rectory's gnarled housekeeper looked in, on her way to bringing Bruck a tray with water glasses. It seemed a little late for that. She winked at me. I grinned back cheerfully and hoped whatever school I'd be attending would offer me adventure books. They'd be in English, so I'd learn it fast. After *The Master of Ballantrae,* maybe more tales by Stevenson—*Treasure Island* or even the sinister *Jekyll and Hyde.*

In particular, I wanted more tales of the Wild West, of regulators and posses like those I'd read about, set in the wilds of Arkansas. I wanted to read about horse thieves, murderers, even corrupt Methodist preachers, and see good and justice triumph, but only after bloodshed and evils grim and dark. I recalled the scene in *The Regulators* where a body, Heathley or Heathscott, was pulled from a frontier river. Slit open by a penknife, its belly was filled with stones, but the body wouldn't stay down.

"Are they expensive?" Father asked bluntly about the parish schools.

"They charge tuition, unlike the public schools. But on your American salary, Herr Kemper—" Bruck broke off and shrugged. "It's a small price to pay."

The meeting ended with great courtesy and the monsignor's blessing. The priest and Father had me join them in the little study for a last goodbye. Fortunately, it was brief, without long spiritual admonitions. Andreas Bruck smiled gamely; if not a choirboy, I was a young man of promise sailing toward opportunity. Afterward, in silence, Father and I left through the library over its creaking floorboards. As we walked toward the stairs, I took one last look around the bookshelves from which I'd been allowed to borrow books on Sunday mornings. Things were serious, all right; we were serious about leaving. Until now, I hadn't thought about the type of school where I'd learn English, but as always, Father seemed determined. Whatever it would be, I'd also learn about America. Somehow, I'd seek out ways to find adventure.

"Did you understand all that, Konrad?" Father said on our way through the overcast square. He meant Monsignor Bruck. In the farmers' co-op, I could see the shoppers crowd the counter for milk and butter, or eggs they sold in twos or threes. We'd already run some last errands. For one thing, someone had told Mother that America had no cuckoo clocks. We'd bought her one as a souvenir of the Austria she'd come to love. As the clocks chimed on the gift shop walls, their cuckoos had made a yodeling sound. Now the package bounced against my knee as I held it by its string.

"Education's serious business," added Father. "Your keys to the kingdom."

He'd never said it quite that way, but I wriggled on the hook as always. "What about these parish schools?"

"We'll have to see," he said. "Time to go finish packing."

His hesitation gave me pause, but this wasn't the time to ask. We had to hurry home before it rained.

The next morning, the chattering gravel truck pulled up at our dingy shack. The driver stayed in the cab, still shy about facing Mother. She hadn't quite forgiven him for running over her prize Leghorn. He left the engine running. Sometimes the quivering truck had trouble starting, even when he turned its crank. Florian Riedl, our friend the lumberjack, jumped from the passenger side to help hoist our bundles up, including Father's proud green trunk with its address in New York, with the *w* spelled as a *v*. Like many German speakers, he mixed up final *v*'s and *w*'s.

We'd sold our little shack below the Alpine peaks to a widow who roomed at a nearby farm. We'd eaten or sold the chickens; the coop and laundry shed stood silent. The hardest thing our last few weeks had been to finish up Mother's keg of sauerkraut. Despite its faint tang of rosemary, even its pleasant burp after eating had become a chore. We had sauerkraut and potatoes morning, noon, and night, even if sometimes with chicken. Finally, Mother had said, "It's done."

"Best kraut I've ever had," said Father, "although never quite this often."

Mother looked fondly at the empty barrel in which the cabbage had marinated. It had been her masterpiece. "It's a good thing you said that. It was a labor of love."

Father laughed.

"You're giving Florian the empty keg?"

"It'll store anything," Father said. "After all he's done for us, no one deserves it more."

For once they agreed wholeheartedly.

Now Florian was back, helping us load our things. Old Fritz Krummbacher, the switchman, came down from his yellow house up the slope by the railroad tracks along with my classmate Berti. I didn't want to see either of them, especially not Berti, the gossip and instigator. We'd already said goodbye at school. But old Fritz had come to shake Father's hand. Berti held back, sullen. I just nodded. Then they both waved goodbye, just as a train for which they'd set the switch came bearing down from the station. For a minute, I thought Berti's eyes swept across the river as if to scout for an army dump truck pulling up.

I wore my thick American coat with its hood in back, just in case it got cold, and jumped up into the truck bed before Father could even hoist me there. He and Mother squeezed into the cab in front between the driver and Florian. There wasn't much more to it than that, as far as I could see. From the back, resting among our chest and bundles, I watched Straubling recede—the pale houses and the countryside, and finally the church spire whose upside-down mirror image seemed to bob in the Salzach River. The river seemed to sing along the graveled road. Above the road in slow motion danced the Alps, towering and magnificent.

CHAPTER 2

NIGHTFALL

I wasn't always that ready. We'd come a long way, although our rough start was no worse than most. The worst thing was saying goodbye to Grandfather, but we escaped Tito's prison camp for Germans like us. We had to leave Grandfather behind; he was old and sick. The road from him led to Austria and eventually to Father, who worked as a farmhand after being released by the Americans. Somehow, he'd found a way to contact Mother in the prison camp. She joined a band of inmates who'd bribed the guards to let them flee toward Hungary.

I'll always remember that fall. The mulberry and chestnut leaves fell red and brown into the dust, and a soft wind drove them through the streets of the camp. Even then, I'd begun to dream of America. Walking with Grandfather in the days before we fled, I'd ask him where it was. He preferred teaching me the alphabet because the camp had no school. When I pestered him, as always, he finally said, "Pretty far. Won't let go, will you?"

I took that as approval. "What's it like?" I asked.

"They say it's big," he said, "and the people aren't hungry."

"Why don't we go there?" I suggested.

"It's dangerous to leave."

"But someday we will?"

"Someday, my boy."

He took my hand as we walked. The wind raised the leaves and turned them in the dust. Two Communist guards with rifles patrolled on the other side of the street. In the meantime Mother secretly got us ready, boiling potatoes and stuffing old clothes in a bundle. I understood we had to flee. At the rate the Communists starved us we wouldn't last the winter. With time the wind grew colder as the remaining leaves fell. The women gathered them for fuel and to sleep on at night.

I'm sure our goodbye was what finally killed Grandfather; it probably broke his heart. When it was time I looked at Mother, itching from the wool stockings she had knitted. Even then she was that mix of daring and irritating practicality. She took the bundled clothing for bribes along with hard cornbread, and I carried our boiled potatoes in a dented tin pail. She began to cry; I guess she had to. Grandfather leaned over me and coughed. He was coughing too much—smoked those damned chestnut leaves. He was practically coughing in my face, but I didn't mind. Soon we crawled out into the dark from under the barbed wire.

A late November frost covered the grass. A child sneezed, and a Serbian guard called out, "*Stoj!*" his hoarse voice like a wolf's. "Stop!" We dropped to the grass, and our guide huddled with the guard. Flecks of white snowed to the ground. The guard cursed over the fallen cigarettes and waved us on. An old Serbian fisherman ferried us across the Tisa River in groups of four and five. As the water splashed against his canoe I clutched the handle of the pail. From within the reeds by the shore came the smell of rotting flesh. "Hurry," whispered the fisherman, but I didn't see Mother in his boat. As I clambered into his canoe I lost the tin lid of the pail. To my relief Mother crossed with the next load.

Nights we trekked north toward Hungary. Our guide left us to escort another group out. As Mother told me years later, it was a way some inmates scavenged to survive. Even the camp's Communist commandant took his cut. We were happy to eat our boiled potatoes as we journeyed north. By day we slept in haystacks and cornfields, making sure to hide in the stubble. We'd walk all night and sometimes lost our way; one morning found we had walked a circle. And that night again we walked. When a child cried out, everyone panicked. But nothing happened—no guards, no guns, no firing. The night was cold and wet, then the darkness spawned a dawn.

We heard roosters in a village and hid till nightfall in a poplar grove. Our stomachs growled, but we walked on with parched mouths and aching backs. An old woman collapsed and asked us to leave her. Although wet from the dew, my woolen stockings scratched and itched, dried on my skin, caught clinging burrs. Ever since I've hated wool. We approached a foggy wood. We heard shooting, then shouts in Serbian. Someone prayed. We inched forward. A baby cried; we heard a shot.

We stumbled through fogged-in ditches, panting and wet. And still I clutched the handle of the bouncing pail. It was empty now, but I held on despite the lost lid. I couldn't see in the fog. The shots resumed, then stopped; the sound of bells moved closer. A dog barked, hoarse and furious. We fell to the dewy grass, expecting border guards. Misty shapes passed near us over wet corn stubble; a breath of cold air carried the smell of sheep and pipe smoke. The sound of bells passed. The dog barked farther on, and the smoking shepherd called out in Hungarian. We rose to breathe. As the swaths of fog lifted, we glimpsed the outlines of a village. It looked like our old hometown, but of course it wasn't. Again the sky dawned in the east, and we heard roosters crow. Somehow we'd crossed the frontier into Hungary.

The women in our band made the rounds of the Hungarian village, making sure to carry hungry children. Mother took me along for the impression. The peasants pitied us and gave us bread and suet. Mother coaxed me to eat slowly. I wouldn't listen and devoured the pork rolled in paprika with chunks of bread. Soon my stomach hurt like everyone's. Our thirst grew violent, and the peasants gave us milk. They pointed out the road to Austria, as if knowing Hungary too would soon turn Communist. When our group broke apart, Mother and I walked on alone. She had a plan; she always had a plan. It included Father, waiting for us in Austria on that farm north of Salzburg.

We rode a peasant's jolting wagon and stowed away on a train, my first of many trains. Night fell across the Hungarian plain. The train had magic and mystery. Rocking in its iron cradle, we didn't yet know we were destined for a refugee camp in Salzburg. First came Father. When we finally saw him, he remarked how thin we were. But as soon as we joined him on Oberbichler's farm, it was clear the farmer had no use for us. We were extra mouths to feed.

Oberbichler didn't want to say it outright, but he scratched his scruffy head. "It can't work, no how," he said stubbornly. "I hired a farmhand, not a family."

Father almost took his head off. We deserted Oberbichler and left him one farmhand short to set out for the city of Mozart. In Salzburg we officially became refugees. It was a promotion of sorts, the move from prison camp to a refugee camp.

CHAPTER 3

THE EMPEROR

That spring in Salzburg, Father nudged me. "That man looks like our old emperor!"

I'd hear much more about him. In 1948, in the meantime, Austria filled up with refugees from Eastern Europe. They called us DPs, displaced persons fleeing from the Communists, many of us ethnic Germans. In this time of charlatans and survivors, refugee camps had leaky roofs, soup rations, women without husbands, and fatherless noisy children. Throughout Austria, the mood seemed grim and hopeless yet somehow not totally serious. It was the war and what came after—the refugees and survivors, broken roads and bridges, ration cards, the trade in smokes or nylons, wilted beets and potatoes, American and Soviet garrisons, and cripples everywhere.

I was probably lucky I had Father to tug at my leash. It was a time for mischief, and I was growing up before my time. I should have been in school, but I was learning plenty. Luckily Grandfather Wendt had planted in me the alphabet and even arithmetic. After Mother and I escaped Yugoslavia, we'd found Father, the former American POW. On Rainer Street close to our camp stood the bombed-out Hotel Europa, and Mozart's birthplace just across the Salzach River.

The Salzburg refugee camp was a transfer point. Refugees huddled in barracks, waited in soup lines, or started Red Cross searches for lost kin. People slept on floors propped up against their bundles or gossiped about the roomier camp upstream to which we might be transferred. Two crippled former soldiers glowered from a corner, playing chess on a cracked board, their crutches idle beside them. One looked up fiercely yet didn't see me. Just then someone cried out. Mother recognized an old couple, Resi and Peter Eberhardt, from our hometown back in Yugoslavia.

"Resi, is that you?" she asked.

Old Resi hugged her in the soup line. "Anni Kemper!"

She pulled old Peter around, who looked at us, astonished. I didn't remember them, but Mother and Father did. Everyone began embracing.

"How did you manage to get out?" Mother asked.

"It was luck, just pure dumb luck," babbled Resi, tears of joy on her cheeks. "We didn't want to go, but next door the Defferts were hitching up their wagon. They had things piled in back and convinced us to join them. It went against our instincts, but Deffert took charge as usual. He always thought he knew better, and this time he did. They didn't want to stay when the East started crumbling. The Red Army had just pushed into Romania—"

"They steamrolled over everything," said Peter Eberhardt dryly, as if spent by Resi's babbling. "Fall 1944, the Germans were exhausted. They didn't care about us. The Russians headed toward us along with Tito's partisans." Peter turned to Father. "But you already know that, Hans, don't you? Our boys were stuck in a German unit. We thought we'd survive the Russians, but the partisans? Deffert said they'd kill us."

"He was right," said Father.

"Most of us wanted to stay," said old Eberhardt. "We thought we had nothing to fear. We avoided politics. And we would have stayed except for Deffert."

"And thank God he knew better," Resi broke in, as usual finishing Peter's sentences. "We joined a column of refugees pushing north. And along the way we started hearing—"

"You missed the worst of it," said Father. "Anni can tell you. Where's Deffert now?"

Resi began crying. "In the end he never made it."

"An old problem with his ticker," Peter said. "On the long road his heart gave out. Strong as an ox, but his ticker, it didn't match his heart. With his family we pushed north anyway and at first ended up near Wels. There was nothing they could do but leave him by the roadside. The Germans wouldn't stop the column."

After that we saw the Eberhardts regularly, with Mother telling Resi about the prison camp. Father and old Peter talked about our hometown those last days before the Russians came. I liked the two, retired from farming until the Germans drafted their sons. Then they had to run their farm again; then both their boys went missing.

Father had put his arm around Peter. "We're lucky to survive. Many never made it." Seeing the old man's wistful look, he added, "But you can't ever give up hope."

I didn't want to hear about more suffering. At least old Peter wasn't shedding tears. Something intervened before he could. As Herr Gruber entered the barracks, Father thought he had found his emperor.

The "emperor" looked magnificent. Even taller than Father, he had a paunch and barrel chest. Like a soldier scouting new terrain, he surveyed the bodies scattered over the barracks floor. His costume was traditional Austrian, a suit of dark gray wool trimmed with green cuffs and lapels. Grizzled sideburns framed his cheeks and rakish handlebars flared over his chin. Below his twinkling eyes his cheeks looked flushed. Father succumbed to this figure from another time.

"That man's the spitting image of our old emperor, Kaiser Franz Josef!"

"Hans, don't stare!" Mother said.

Father got swept up in the emperor's military strut. "He's advancing toward us!"

As a baby squalled, the emperor strode toward our quieter patch of floor. I looked him over top to bottom but thought I liked Father more. Already Father was a mystery to me, who favored discipline but chuckled over human lapses. He rose to extend his hand toward the emperor.

"Hans Kemper," he introduced himself.

"Gruber. Franz Gruber," intoned the emperor.

Although they'd just met, they shook hands like long-lost army pals. Father pulled Herr Gruber toward Mother, who peeped a stiff hello. The emperor's hands were flecked with age spots, and his handlebars looked tobacco-stained. I got a good look at him, but then, like the Eberhardts, they turned to refugee talk. Where the emperor was from, what country we had called home, when Herr Gruber had fled, when we did. The usual litany. When his name had turned out to be Franz, like the Austrian emperor's, Father winked at me. It added fuel to his fire.

In the meantime it took weeks for the barracks to be partitioned. That led to an encounter that brought Father and the emperor closer yet. Herr Gruber had gone for a walk but forgotten his pipe. Returning to the deserted barracks, he spotted a refugee rummaging through our bundles.

"What do you think you're doing, mud rat?" thundered the emperor.

The thief shrank against the walls as Herr Gruber charged him with his cane. He escaped by the far door. Father was touched to hear about it.

"That sorry piece of trash almost got my canteen," he said. "After all the years I held on to it. It's got some dents, but not one hole was ever shot through it!" The wide-mouthed canteen was standard German issue to soldiers in the field.

"The Nazis forced us to soldier," Father added, "but I got attached to it. Things never looked too bleak as long as I had scraps in it. Now that scum tore up our bags tugging at my damned canteen!" Pausing for effect, he spread out his large hands. "Just let me get my hands on him!"

Herr Gruber nodded vehemently. "Exactly. People just aren't how they were."

Luckily for the thief, Father never caught up with him. But after this I began to ask him about our Emperor Franz and got more details than I'd wanted.

Herr Gruber had lost his farm in the Sudetenland, the German-speaking region in what had become Czechoslovakia. After World War I its German speakers, once part of Austria-Hungary, suddenly became Czech nationals, but apparently most still thought of themselves as German. And so, Father said, in 1938 Hitler annexed the territory. But once the Nazis retreated at the end of World War II, the Czechs killed or expelled many of the Sudeten Germans. Herr Gruber had fled with Erna, his daughter.

We, in the meantime, had lost our farm in Yugoslavia to Tito's Communists. They equated German speakers with fascists although we had lived there for two centuries, from the time it was Hungarian and Austrian and long before it ever became Yugoslavia. It was not a good time to be heard speaking German in Eastern Europe.

But Father and the emperor had even much more in common. Herr Gruber's wife had died before the war, and like many refugees, he now looked for next of kin. During their flight, he'd somehow lost his daughter, Erna, while Mother and Father sought two brothers we never found.

Despite this or because of the war, Father and the emperor spoke fondly of discipline and of soldiering, especially the bygone *K.u.K.,* the Austro-Hungarian imperial army in which Herr Gruber had once served as a corporal. And Father had been conscripted by the Germans invading Yugoslavia.

And always, as they talked, Herr Gruber remained the spitting image of Francis Joseph I, Austria's last Hapsburg emperor. In fact the only time Father ever openly lost his sense of humor was when he spat the word *Yugoslavia,* which he viewed as an affront created by the victors of World War I as a reward for their Serb allies. Only Austria-Hungary was real to him, with Herr Gruber its last emperor.

CHAPTER 4

A TOUCHING SYMMETRY

In time even I got to know the emperor. The refugee camp lacked a school, and we had lice, but Father had me writing little essays on camp life just to keep my hand in. When I wrote up his canteen, he barely held back a grin. With all my questions, luckily he proved almost as patient as Grandfather Wendt. One evening he even taught me how to tell the waxing from the waning moon. It was a memory trick using the first letters of the German words for *wax* and *wane.*

I was impressed but not unduly. I still needed more to pass the time and began to sneak out to stalk Herr Gruber on his rounds. Before his walks the emperor would brush his coat and twirl his handlebars. That was my signal. The first day I lost him among the sour pedestrians on Rainer Street near the ruined Hotel Europa, partly due to another refugee, a boy named Norbert. He had round green eyes and red hair and breathed through his mouth, and I could never quite shake him off. Just then he chose to stick his tongue out. It looked pale green.

I gave him back the raspberry. He didn't look impressed.

By now I'd lost the emperor. But two days later I tracked him to the Mirabell Gardens. He looked at home among the stately chestnut trees. As he paraded down its shady lanes and graveled paths, he twirled his cane and sometimes pressed it to the ground. Then he would swing it up toward his left hand, pluck its tip, and flick something toward his pocket. Smoke curled from his pipe as he strode past benches and dour women with shopping nets foraging for bread or potatoes.

I crept closer. Once more the emperor dropped his cane, then swung it high and toward his left. I saw a white blur on its tip. So that was it. The emperor speared cigarette butts from the graveled ground. The cane's tip held a nail he'd filed into a spike. His dignity would not let him stoop.

Right off I decided to help him.

I rolled a scrap of newspaper into a paper cone and began to stalk the gardens, like him studying the ground for stubs. The Mirabell Gardens were a refuge and everyone's favorite passage, with the majestic castle on the hill as a backdrop. If you looked hard, you could find cigarettes smoked down to the nub and discarded almost anywhere. On some you could make out the faint word *Camel.* Engrossed as I collected, I lost track of the emperor. But later I spied him on a park bench.

The result of his labors piled beside him, he studied his stubs with affection. He pared off their ashen tips with a pocket knife, trimming close to save precious tobacco, then cleaned the paper from the stubs and fluffed up the tiny tobacco wads. He loaded his pipe with fresh tobacco and stored the rest in old newspaper. His handlebars quivered as he lit his pipe and smoked. Our Emperor Franz was happy.

It took daring to interrupt him. "Herr Gruber," I somehow managed, "I thought—do you think these butts are still good?"

The emperor set his pipe down in dismay. I pushed my offering toward him. His jaws looked about to drop, but I couldn't be sure due to his handlebars. His hand reached out to pat my shoulder. "This is good of you, my little friend," he too finally managed. "You have your father's lion heart!"

The rest of that spring and summer, I collected stubs for the emperor. We had an understanding. Soon after, however, we were finally transferred to a less crowded refugee camp upstream from Salzburg. The city overflowed with refugees.

The layout of our new camp in Straubling, like Salzburg in the American zone, had a kind of symmetry. The Salzach River divided the town in two as it flowed north toward Salzburg, with our barracks pasted on the river's left. Straubling's church and school and market square lay clustered in the hills on the right bank. To its north and south, two bridges flung across the river connected the halves. Around us in all directions rose the peaks of the Alps. The mountains toward the north were snowy Alpine jewels that barred us from the city of Mozart. It was picture postcard scenery, hopefully with some scraps to eat.

Our barracks turned out to be a former German army warehouse and later dance hall for a contingent of Serb Royalist officers who like us had fled Tito's Communists. Their garrison across the river adjoined that of the Americans. The drafty warehouse was Straubling's contribution to our welfare. What I didn't yet know was that Herr Gruber would literally join us.

The trees were already changing colors as our train ground to a stop. Down the corridor a stocky refugee built like a chimney offered to help the crippled former soldiers with their bundles—the two I'd seen playing chess. They proudly refused his offer. Another, a slender refugee, surprisingly in shirt and tie, looked on with mock pity. I'd know the shyster later. As Father hustled us out of our second-class compartment and down to the railroad tracks, he laughed and shook me by the scruff of the neck. "Time to start your schooling, rascal. Your brain's itching for a home."

Almost as soon as we'd arrived in Straubling we heard from the Eberhardts, our friends in Salzburg. More refugees from Yugoslavia had just reached the city, among them Lenschi Kleitsch. She was among the fortunate ones who, with a married daughter in Cleveland in the state of Ohio, would probably soon get to America. She had news that we'd expected, but it shook Mother. Grandfather Wendt was dead.

He'd died the fall we escaped, during a typhus epidemic that swept the prison camp. The cold and his smoking didn't help. In our warehouse of a barracks, we'd just put up some sheets as a temporary partition, and that evening Mother sat below them as she held the note from the Eberhardts. The letter shook her like a small convulsion. Father put his arms around her. I didn't know what to do, and that night I couldn't sleep. The next morning, without a word, Mother went uptown to look for work.

I began to miss Grandfather Wendt when my new teacher at the grammar school, Fräulein Seebach, tacked her graceful letters of the alphabet on a long, wide strip of paper that ran high up all around our classroom walls. Grandfather's letters had been more angular but just as clear as hers.

As I started school, it began to snow in the foothills.

CHAPTER 5

A HEART FOR REFUGEES

The two invalids looked bitter but superior. Like all of us, they would share a narrow partition in our former warehouse. Even before I started school, our first order of business was to build those partitions. In Salzburg we'd been told that in our new camp each family would have its separate space. But as we found out, it was up to us to scrounge up the lumber. In the drafty warehouse and former dance hall for the Serbian Royalists, Father once again took things into his own hands.

He found some scrap planks through Florian Riedl, a local lumberjack whom he'd helped build a shed. Once he started hammering our partition everyone wanted in. Stocky Sepp Blassmann got boards too and began to work them. As on the train earlier, he again offered to help the crippled former soldiers. Unlike the two invalids, the Royalists we met later had escaped Yugoslavia with their limbs intact, but the two of them worked fiercely on their own. One of them, Ludwig, even looked like a carpenter, joining scrap lumber so seamlessly it looked like real walls.

In the meantime Father and Blassmann helped the widowed mothers. For a while woodpeckers seemed to tap everywhere, although summer was long past. But even when we had our partitions up, an icy draft rose from gaps in the floor boards, and the wooden partitions let you hear everything on the other side.

Despite this, some refugees glued brown packing paper over the boards with a paste of water and flour. Slimy Franz and Ludwig, as Mother called the one-legged soldiers, took the housekeeping one step further. On the paper they penciled a loving rosary of female behinds. From the beginning, their chess and drawings pulled me in.

I learned plenty, but soon school was my next project. The day the new school year opened Father enrolled me with gusto. The gray schoolhouse rose just behind the church. Even within its grove of chestnut trees you could see it needed paint and stucco, although it looked better when it snowed. Somehow Father persuaded Arnold Vogt, the director, to move me up a grade despite my being a refugee. Circumstances beyond my control, he insisted. Besides, I knew the basics. Moving up a grade would still leave me one year short of where I should have been.

"And his age?" asked Vogt, superior.

"Nine," said Father.

He showed Vogt my essays about the Hotel Europa, Herr Gruber, and the Mozart House, and Vogt reconsidered. He consulted Fräulein Seebach, my likely teacher in the second grade. My earnest essays must have struck her, if not the shaky spelling. I looked eager. She agreed.

"Then it's settled," said Vogt, baring his yellow teeth, seeming satisfied he'd done his duty. "We'll make him a good Austrian."

Out of the corner of my eye I saw Father lurch. More important, he'd gained me a year. The other refugee children also started school, mixed in with Austrians, but in another room and mostly in first grade. In room 2c I was the lone refugee. But though I was older than my classmates, I was no bigger, so at first I kept my mouth shut.

As we left Vogt, Father put his large hand on my shoulder. "You're a Kemper. We start out small, but we fill out."

That helped reconcile me to my size. Fortunately I soon liked school and Fräulein Seebach, who became my guardian angel. Some classmates called us DPs, but mostly school turned out full of good surprises, not least our teacher. Inge Seebach came from an established local family. Patient and kindly, for some reason she had a heart for refugees. She made school into a refuge in our world of scavengers and survivors. To her all of us were special, even Gustl Ponkratz.

One morning she surprised us. I'd just discovered the old atlas on a shelf behind our desks and itched to study it. It was just a few weeks to Christmas, and a fragrant pine wreath with white candles hung from the ceiling to mark the season. As it snowed outside, Fräulein Seebach took a paper tissue from her purse to blow her nose. We looked up, astonished. And then she threw the tissue out.

It was a time for colds, but a paper handkerchief you threw away was beyond our comprehension. Handkerchiefs were meant to be reused. We barely heard her words.

"Let's take our recess, children," she announced. "I'll return in a minute."

As soon as she left, the room erupted. We didn't have much by way of snacks, but recess gave us license. Everyone chattered about the tissue—the fact she'd used it and then dropped it in her wastebasket. She could have reused it once, at least. Where did she get them? What merchant dared to stock them? The idea could only have come from America, probably from the garrison by the riverbank. "Could it be," dared someone, I think our gossip Berti Krummbacher, "she has an American friend?"

We fell silent. Almost as quickly Gustl Ponkratz, the butcher's son, managed to drop a wedge of ripe cheese on the hot classroom radiator. It figured. Gustl was probably the only one who could even afford this smelly cheese. Deep down, I think he wanted to rub our noses in it. Soon its stink floated everywhere. The boys snickered in their glee to despise Gustl. The girls guarded a noble silence, but Susi Palfner wrinkled her nose the way she did at refugees. Only Monika Waldegger, the pretty one, looked embarrassed. I wasn't to blame and shrugged right back at her.

As the snow flurried outside, the radiator steamed with heat. The cheese smell rose from it as melting goo seeped deep into its coils. You couldn't open the windows; they'd bring in icy air. It was a *quark,* as I recall, sticky squares you normally bought in rolls of five or six. The fact you bought them in a store meant Gustl's family had money. The question remained, had he done it on purpose, or was he just stupid enough to drop the cheese accidentally to drip into the radiator's coils?

"He's too much of an idiot," surmised Herbert Mautner, "to do it intentionally."

Gustl cowered like a worried rabbit, holding his half-eaten bun.

"Or even accidentally on purpose," scoffed Berti Krummbacher, the railroad switchman's son. "Unless someone put him up to it."

Herbert towered over him. "Was it you?"

"What are you saying?" Berti squawked. "I have to breathe the stink same as you. Could someone from another class have put him up to it, maybe from 2a? They don't actually have to smell it."

Gustl's rabbit eyes darted between them.

"We should rub his nose in it," said Rupert Bichlhofer, whose father's farm stood next to Palfner's in the foothills above our camp.

"Quiet," hushed someone. "Fräulein Seebach's back."

CHAPTER 6

THE ATLAS

By now the stink of Gustl's cheese had journeyed to all corners of the classroom, into every desk and pencil box, and begun to envelop the fragrant Christmas wreath suspended from the ceiling. It masked the wreath's pine scent. All eyes turned to Fräulein Seebach to see how the smell would test her. We thought her head jerked back.

"What happened?" she said softly.

"Fräulein Seebach," sniffed Susi Palfner, "someone dropped some cheese—"

"On the radiator," completed Rupert.

Our teacher looked around the room and saw Gustl cowering. "And I believe I know just who." She wouldn't name the culprit, but she called on Gustl. "I need volunteers to clean up. Go to the washroom, Gustl, and find us a rag and water basin."

A relieved Gustl scurried out. When he didn't come back she sent Herbert Mautner after him. Herbert returned with an enamel basin, with Gustl trotting after him holding a damp rag. His face looked raw; Herbert must have massaged it. We all began to scrub the radiator, hoping to keep the cheese from melting deeper into its accordion coils. Rupert Bichlhofer and Gustl even scraped with their pencil points.

But we knew the smell would linger, maybe the rest of winter, unless somehow any trapped cheese would eventually crust and flake out. We completely forgot about our teacher's paper tissues, but the scrubbing used up our recess and continued into grammar hour. Soon we feared losing our lunch hour and itched to run outside to throw snowballs. Gustl scraped anxiously as if in atonement. "The shit," hissed Berti Krummbacher. "Let's cook his goose the way he cooked his cheese."

Finally Fräulein Seebach said, "Thank you, children; that's enough."

She still refused to name the perpetrator.

"That's all we can do for now. Let's be more careful in the future."

We surged out for lunch and snowballs. Lunch meant bowls of polenta in the school basement, probably from a UN charity. Even Gustl joined the line as if to show solidarity. He could have brought buns packed with meat and cheese, just like at recess. Monika Waldegger stood in line before me, her pigtails in my face, as Berti jostled me from behind. She received her bowl politely and thanked the cook, Frau Hackl. I almost got to sit down next to her, but Rupert Bichlhofer eagerly waved her over. They ate and chattered below framed pictures of Austrian peasant costumes.

Outside I threw my snowballs hard. I hit Rupert in the face, dodged one of his, then joined up with Herbert Mautner to bombard Berti. The sport worked off our lunch of cornmeal, and back in the warm classroom none of us even got sleepy.

As if to startle us fully awake, Fräulein Seebach announced, "Soon, children, we may be joined by classmates from room 2a. Frau Klein is going on leave. The rest of her class will temporarily join 2b. They'll be with Herr Faber."

Our jaws dropped.

"We'll be a little cramped here in 2c. But it's a chance to make new friends."

As Herbert Mautner calmly digested the news, Gustl looked alarmed. I looked at the rabbit with distaste, as if this news was somehow tied to the stink from his cheese. I already had enemies in 2a, a classroom next to us; two were Gustl's country cousins. To those farm boys I was a *zugroasta*, a lousy refugee. Besides, I was doing well in school, and being a year older, felt I did it on false pretenses. I wished for the Kemper growth spurt Father had promised. As I pondered Fräulein Seebach's words, Gustl squirmed at his oak desk. First he looked at Herbert Mautner as if to seek permission.

"Fräulein Seebach, can I be excused?"

She understood the danger. "Come back as quickly as you can. We'll be discussing Straubling and our history. You wouldn't want to miss it."

Gustl hurried to the washroom. Cheese or not, he always looked nervous. Rupert Bichlhofer squirmed in mockery, and Inge Seebach had that curious way of smiling, as if amused but didn't want to show it. The cheese smell, in the meantime, clouded the room and seemed to steam the windowpanes.

Gustl got back just in time for a little science lesson on Straubling's butcher shops and the cow's four stomachs. As a butcher's son himself he raised his hand, and Fräulein Seebach gave him his chance to shine. Breathing heavily, he rattled off all gaseous four: rumen, reticulum, omasum, and abomasum. It was so astonishing we almost clapped, except that Fräulein Seebach looked too earnest.

Speaking of cows, I wondered about Gustl's cheese. Did it go with his rye bread? I was sure it filled you up. It probably filled you up much better than the bread with jam some of my classmates brought for snacks. It couldn't really taste as foul as it smelled, or would Gustl eat it? It might even help me start the Kemper growth spurt.

I almost heard Father say, "It's inevitable; you're a Kemper."

For now I was just thin, always looking out for things to eat.

"And now it's time," I heard our teacher say, "for our first lesson in geography."

I leaped to attention. She had me get out the old atlas I'd found in back. It promised a bigger world than local merchants or cow guts. It was a massive, dog-eared volume, Wagner's *Methodical School Atlas* from 1903. I didn't know how it had survived the war without being lost until, inside its front cover, I saw the name Heinrich Seebach in old Gothic script. Fräulein Seebach must have brought it, as a family heirloom.

Its maps were dated, but our classroom had no recent atlas, just one global pull-down map with a tiny Europe. Her *Methodical Atlas* had maps in wonderful faded colors. She opened it to one that looked familiar—a full page of Central Europe. Inge Seebach had us gather around her to study it.

"Let's start with a little history."

Father's own histories had whetted my appetite. Knowing Herr Gruber and Austria-Hungary, I easily picked things out. Squeezing between Fräulein Seebach and Herbert Mautner, I saw all points right side up. Vienna radiated out from the Danube, upstream from Hungary, with the Balkans east and south. My hometown was too small to show, but I spotted Temeschwar. On this old map it was part of Austria-Hungary, like Salzburg and even Straubling. The Tisa River we'd crossed at night meandered south toward Belgrade and the Danube. As yet there was no Yugoslavia, just a small patch of Serbia along one margin. Father would have been delighted. My eyes moved greedily northeast, toward Bohemia and Herr Gruber's Sudetenland.

Most of my classmates didn't know what it all meant, but I could tell Herbert Mautner knew exactly. But although I stood right next to him, I didn't hear him say a word. Instead Rupert Bichlhofer found a dot on the upper reaches of the Salzach River. "There's Salzburg," he said eagerly.

"Exactly!" said Fräulein Seebach. "Can anyone find Straubling?"

She let us hunt. Finally Herbert said, unsurprised, "We're too small."

"An honest answer." Our teacher smiled. "But only as far as numbers. To us it's far bigger, isn't it? And what country do you see?"

"Austria," beamed Rupert.

Berti Krummbacher seemed annoyed that he knew.

"Austria-Hungary, to be exact," added Fräulein Seebach. "The empire of Austria-Hungary, the way we used to be."

A sigh went through the room.

Suddenly I heard my own voice. "Can we see America?" I croaked hoarsely.

Fräulein Seebach looked at me gently. "We'll get to it soon enough, Konrad. Be patient. First the old world, then the new."

I felt myself flush.

That evening, back in camp, the emperor seemed more real than ever. On the way I had passed the invalids' partition and through their half-open curtain saw Franz and Ludwig playing chess. When Father returned from shoveling snow off the railroad tracks, we ladled our rations of black bean soup. I ate hungrily. I could tell Herr Gruber was hungry too. His handlebar mustache quivered when I mentioned the atlas. Suddenly we all talked about the old Austria-Hungary—its expanse and vast domains.

CHAPTER 7

THE COCOON

The day I tripped Gustl Ponkratz, it was a lot of things—his smelly cheese, the cow's four stomachs, and now his thick crisp bun. He paraded it at recess, crammed with meat and cheese. As he was about to stuff his face, I stuck my leg out almost before I knew it. That tripped him just as he pranced between two rows of desks with the bun raised in one hand. His fall sent pencil boxes clattering to the floor, and his nose gushed with blood.

Of all people only our teacher saw me do it. Fräulein Seebach's look shamed me. "How could you, Konrad?"

She almost couldn't believe I'd done it. I didn't feel contrite exactly, only sorry that she'd seen me. She liked me, and I'd disappointed her. Luckily she never told Father, as if she knew what he would do. They'd met that first day of school when Arnold Vogt decided to move me up a grade and make me a good Austrian. Maybe it was as if, by telling Father, she'd have to admit her misplaced confidence. Or maybe she was too surprised to pass him the news. I began to see her as an ally.

The rest of that winter I'd notice Father's big hands when he came home from shoveling snow, hungry for our hot soup. My thoughts were my worst punishment. But Gustl never told, either. We'd learned a lesson. I saw my own stupidity. I never tripped him again, and he never again showed off his snacks. We shared a dirty secret that from now on would keep us clean.

But something else happened as if in retribution—the class merger promised by Fräulein Seebach. A light snow drifted down when some of the boys from 2a joined us. Their arrival distracted me from brooding, but I didn't like it. I had those enemies in 2a—Naz Greiner and Poldi Stiegl. One morning there they sat—Gustl's country cousins.

Naz and Poldi glared at me, hating my foreign guts. For the first few days, at least, they'd be on good behavior. With Inge Seebach's talent for conciliating, they'd be wise to learn some manners. At least they weren't with their buddies from 2a, to be able to plot together. And I couldn't smell them due to Gustl's lingering fumes of melted cheese. But having tripped up Gustl now seemed dumber than ever. I recalled Fräulein Seebach's dismay just when I needed allies. They were Gustl's cousins, and blood was thicker than water.

Walking back to our camp that afternoon I clenched my fists. You couldn't get through to those farm boys. They'd probably never have a fancy cheese like Gustl, although the three were cousins. Naz and Poldi were poor slobs like most of us, whether refugees or locals, just two more mouths to feed, farm boys from the hills above Straubling helping their families scratch out a living.

We'd already notched one run-in, even before they joined our class. Despising any whiff of foreigners, after school they'd caught up with me behind the church. Naz slurred his insults. Then Poldi got behind me and tripped me into a snowbank. Naz fell on top of me, and as Poldi pinned my legs, he twined his thick arms around my neck. I struggled hard, but he locked me in a sweatbox. I got the full benefit of his farm smells—buttermilk, old cheese, manure—as layers in his patched sweater starched with ancient sweat. He pinned my face in the snowbank and slowly ground it raw. Luckily a teacher happened by and pulled us all up by the ears. The meddler Klamm was outraged, but this time I didn't mind.

"Fighting right by the church! Move your sorry hides before I tell your folks."

We slunk off, an unholy trio. With Georg Klamm still watching, I hurried to put distance between myself and Gustl's cousins as outrage ticked inside me. Out of Klamm's sight, safely outside Frau Hollinger's bakery where I could duck in if needed, I gestured at them in defiance. Naz slurred the standard insult for refugees.

"Don't worry, *zugroasta*. We'll just settle up next time."

Reliving the indignity days later, I heard Berti Krummbacher's voice snicker behind me. "Know the latest?"

"What do you know that I don't?" I wasn't in the mood, but he always had the latest gossip. It mattered for survival.

"Lots," he bragged. "Ingrid Klein, from your neck of the woods."

"What about her? Fräulein Seebach said she'd be on leave." Frau Klein, the teacher, was a refugee from Romania. I figured Berti had another shoe to drop.

"Seems that knowing how to swear in four languages isn't the end of her skills."

"What do you know about languages?"

"Took off, disappeared. Ran off with one of your king's men, one of those Serb goons from the garrison. The freeloaders planning to save the Balkans."

Damn, he'd trumped me. Even if only half of all that was true, that evening our camp would buzz with this gossip. And Naz and Poldi might join our class indefinitely, to stick in my craw. That evening I heard Berti's rumor confirmed.

The next day after school I consulted Herbert Mautner. Unlike Gustl Ponkratz, he was big and steady, in case anyone tried to get me. If Berti was our gossip, Herbert was the weary cynic.

"What do you think?" I asked. "Did Ingrid Klein run off for keeps?"

"One of the Royalists, I heard. She saw her chance, maybe her last one. True love, whatever. My father said, 'Who'd have had her?'"

"How would he know?"

"From the district court. Sometimes he's a liaison for the Americans. The Serbs are military too. The fellow's name is Zoran Zarić. You can probably say it better."

"Never heard of him."

"Thought you might have, being from there. There's something else."

We passed Straubling's cemetery. "What's that?"

"There's an American. But not a peep to anyone."

"Of course not," I said.

"Another of your exotic types, dark hair and pencil mustache. Even parts his hair down the middle. If not for that, could just as easily pass for a slick Viennese *strizi.* Maybe he's one of their Spaniards, although his name sounds English. Berti was right. This Curtis Bishop's courting Fräulein Seebach."

More bad news. I could be losing my one patron—the teacher who liked me. My thoughts raced; she might even leave before us.

"How can that be?" I asked Herbert.

"Balkan gigolos, Spaniards, Yanks, whatever. Whatever they carry, it might be contagious."

"You're making fun of me."

"Just saying. It's where she gets those tissues."

Herbert must have gotten that gossip from his father too. It must have been where he'd learned words like *gigolo*, hearing his father talk about the court. Now Herbert mentioned our instructor in religion class.

"If Simon Dachnagl knew, he'd probably excommunicate her. The American could be anything, even a Baptist or Methodist. Fräulein Seebach's staunchly Catholic. Beyond that, it's all respectable. You know she's on the up-and-up. But in the end, she probably won't have him."

We had passed the shops and chestnut trees and neared the town's residential part, where the road dwindled to a path down toward the Salzach River and our camp below.

"Want to stop by?" Herbert ended. "I have an article that'll interest you."

"What did you say his name was?"

"Who, the American? Curtis Bishop."

I didn't like the sound of it. "Where's he from?"

"Texas, I think. It's the Prussia of America."

I envisioned pencil mustaches. Serbian or American, they were suspect. I'd have to keep my ears open. Anyway, Herbert said I'd find his article interesting.

He lived in a regular house with rooms. The article turned out to be one he'd clipped from a newspaper, a stifling tale of three German soldiers buried when American planes bombed a city. Luckily for them, when the bombs hit they were sheltered in a bakery cellar where their sergeant had sent them to look for food. The cellar became their tomb. It contained tubs of flour, and moisture trickled through the rubble that they could lap off the walls. They could even channel it into barrels when water streamed down during rains. But it was totally black inside—they found just two candles—and they were buried too deep to be heard above ground. In the end they survived months and years on a gruel of water and flour. It was probably like the sticky paste we used in camp to glue paper over the pine partitions. I doubt they dreamed about America, as I'd started doing.

Then time began to pick them off. Despite the unending flour, they got scurvy and weakened. One died of a fever. The second soldier went crazy after helping bury the dead man in a tub of flour. He died a babbling bag of bones and skin. Finally, almost three years after their burial, the last survivor heard machinery far above lift bricks and rubble as workers started to rebuild the broken city. When they found him, he was lucid but blinded by the sunlight. No photograph came with the article, but I imagined him propped up in a steel-frame hospital bed as he whispered to reporters, his skin like brittle parchment and his eyes glinting like a mole's.

It was a story made for our cynic, Herbert, who was a sponge for words like *gigolo* or *accidentally on purpose*. Our class thought one day he'd be a surgeon. He had just discovered the word *irony*, so this story was a feast.

I didn't want to disappoint him, but I almost gagged. As always, food was on my mind. Thinking of that rancid paste of water and flour, I almost lost my appetite. Compared to the trapped soldiers I felt lucky, but I must have hurt Herbert's feelings when I said I'd just as soon sniff Gustl's cheese.

In the meantime, somehow I couldn't say the same for Herr Gruber. He wasn't lucky; even I could see it coming. When we got to Straubling, after offering to let him share our partition, at first Father had managed to calm Mother about the emperor. She washed his sheets and warmed his soup along with ours. His bunk stood squeezed along one wall of our tiny space, and she seemed to accept our lack of privacy. There wasn't much of it for anyone—just sheets and clothes hung within as dividers, and the wood partitions. I slept in the window bunk above Mother and Father. Luckily none of us snored, except the emperor slightly. I wasn't sure Father believed it, but he claimed the arrangement would be temporary.

One day he told me how it came about. Just before our transfer from Salzburg to the camp in Straubling, his friendship with Herr Gruber had reached a high point. We'd been told, falsely as I said, that each family was to have its own partition. In a burst of camaraderie, Father invited Herr Gruber to join us, as a "family member" so to speak. Mother was aghast. But already Father and the emperor shook hands warmly. After the dislocations and turmoil of the war and what followed, their friendship seemed like destiny. Herr Gruber must have needed human contact. Yet he tactfully asked Mother how she felt.

"I must leave it up to you, Frau Kemper," he said, courtly. "We men often strike bargains, but I'm afraid it's you who might be burdened."

Mother could see how much Father wanted to help Herr Gruber. But although she liked the emperor, she harbored a taint of practicality. She thought their bargain would burden all of us, even the emperor. Herr Gruber had foreseen it. What probably bothered her most was that Father hadn't consulted her. But she seemed aware that he needed to assert a kinder side, or he would be unhappy and maybe less of a father. So she shielded both of us. If things backfired she could always say, "I told you so."

"Yes, Herr Gruber," she said vaguely. "Who knows what the future will bring?"

"There, you see?" Father told the emperor.

For a while that seemed to settle things.

CHAPTER 8

TWO KNIGHTS

Outside the snow fell steadily, muffling sound inside the barracks. The season's biggest storm made the foothills disappear along with Palfner's farm; Lechner's fields and downstream barn were gone. I liked winter, the way it changed everything.

"What did you say your name was?" Ludwig said, although by now he should have known.

"Konrad," I said.

His crutches stood to one side. "So you like chess?"

"I'd like to play like you."

"You're how old, did you say?"

What did age have to do with it? "Ten," I said, so they would let me watch. I'd first seen them play in Salzburg, long before I really watched their games.

"Good age to start."

"Sit down; you're tempting fate," interrupted Franz, the left-legged player. He huddled in a faded Wehrmacht coat with the insignia ripped off.

Ludwig, the one I thought the artist, seemed to pay him no attention. He pondered his next move, then sprung a deadly trap. Pushing his black bishop forward to attack Franz's queen, he simultaneously unveiled his rook. The rook's discovered check allowed his bishop to capture the queen. Franz should have seen it coming. Surveying the battle lines, Ludwig looked up and growled.

"Shut the door and sit," he seconded Franz. "You make me nervous standing there on two good legs, like that."

I didn't like his tone but felt compelled to watch. I moved inside their grimy partition, muffling the children's shoes rattling across the wooden floor. A draft rose from cracks between the floorboards, despite the crumpled newspaper stuffed in them.

The two invalids played chess day in and out. I didn't know their last names until finally Mother told me. She said the names in disgust although she usually took my side. They were camp outsiders and never thought to introduce themselves. Only their chess seemed to matter to them. Unlike the few able-bodied men in the refugee camp, like Father or Sepp Blassmann, being cripples they didn't shovel snow off railroad tracks. It was the only work that winter. Refugees didn't get first crack at real jobs, only the locals did—the loggers and the farmhands. During winter that meant shoveling, not collecting unemployment. Austria first took care of its own, not refugees like us. But amputees couldn't even shovel snow; they lacked the legs for leverage.

Between them, of course, Franz and Ludwig had two good ones. That wouldn't do—one reason why I think they played. Over time they'd lost their two white knights, and they lacked one king. So they kneaded two white knights and a king from rye bread to replace them. Their chess board was chipped and grimy, but you could still tell the dark squares from the light. Father thought they'd survived the war because they'd been wounded early, each losing a healthy leg. They never talked about it, although it must have mattered to them. Surly Franz had lost his right leg; Ludwig the artist lost his left. It didn't seem to matter who lost which. They both looked sullen as they played into the nights, sustained by all that cheek. That was their other thing. They had the time, unlike Father and Sepp Blassmann, who shoveled snow off the railroad tracks. At the war's end it seemed important for the winter trains to run on time.

"Damn you," Franz finally said. "You're playing inspired chess."

Staring at their board, I awoke from my thoughts.

Ludwig glowered at the board, his lips drawn, as though wanting to rip hearts out. "It's the kid; he brings me luck."

"I'm just meat today," Franz growled back.

"You should have seen that coming."

"You've had me on the run, just trying to survive."

"Do you want to play, or talk?"

Franz turned on me instead. "Close that door tightly, kid."

The door was warped, made of those scrap planks from Florian Riedl, with bark still on the edges. I tried to pull it tight but could still hear the children run. The brown packing paper glued over their boards was too thin. Even though they'd made a door, not just hung a sheet, Franz and Ludwig seemed impatient like everyone. I just wanted to play like Ludwig. But as the stronger and more talented, he probably also had those other moves. I mean the drawings on their papered walls, lovingly rendered plump behinds. The pencil strokes caressed their cheeks with just a hint of trunks or thighs.

Mother despised the two, but Father merely shrugged. "Idle barracks humor. When soldiers can't, they dream." He winked at me.

Something interesting was in that wink. "What do you mean?" I asked.

"Never mind," said Mother angrily. "Disgusting, this camp. The vile things it exposes children to."

"You're right, but just think," he said. "Those poor bastards can't even shovel."

Luckily they'd asked me inside to watch, so Mother couldn't see us. The draft rose through their floor boards. I didn't mind the naked flesh, but I loved the technique. Something inside me was beginning to shift not just toward chess, but toward this art called drawing. I liked drawing hour in school and rendering things I loved. It was one reason it was fascinating to study Fräulein Seebach's methodical atlas.

Now Ludwig's queen, backed by his rook, captured Franz's white knight, a mere fig leaf trying to protect his king. Crunched to the edge of the board, his white king was dead. Ludwig threw the dried-out, shriveled king toward the other captured pieces on his cot. Although kneaded of rye bread, it clattered like wood.

"Checkmate," he said.

Franz threw one crutch into a corner. That gave me pause. Losing was bad enough, but having to rely on crutches was worse. You'd have to ease your way through doorways, leaning forward as you nudged doors open with your crutch. But just about anything might go wrong. If someone in a hurry suddenly barged through from the other side as you surged forward, you could fall right on your face, unless whoever did the barging reacted just in time to jerk you up. But if the other person was a woman, she might not have the strength. You might even fall on top of her. Actually that might not bother Franz or Ludwig if Father gauged their dreams correctly.

Doors weren't the only challenge, either, because most people now were irritable. They weren't inclined to help with opening doors or anything. In the refugee camp and throughout Austria, as I said, it was those leaky roofs, scrawny mothers without husbands, and those fatherless noisy brats. It was the war and what came after—refugees and survivors, broken bridges, ruined hotels and cratered roads; it was the rationing, moldy beets and potatoes, garrisons of all kinds, and crippled former soldiers everywhere, like Franz and Ludwig. And if a woman would have them, as Father had implied, she'd be having half a man.

As Mother said, the things you learned in camp. Now I saw Franz the loser glare at me. "You take him on," he told Ludwig.

"What?" I said, startled.

"You're ready, kid. You've been watching us like a hawk every chance you get. You're just about his lucky charm. You'll never be readier. Time to show us what you've got." He paused, laughing hoarsely. "Now it's your ass on the line."

I paled, but I was flattered. They kept saying "kid," even though they knew my name and age. Vainly seeking comfort, my eyes darted around their walls of lovingly crafted behinds. The rosary of drawings looked to be at a level reached comfortably by a man doodling from his cot. Could it be Franz who was really the artist? Or did nature unfairly grant Ludwig both chess and art?

"Set 'em up," commanded Ludwig.

The children had stopped running, and the falling snow muffled our words. The newspaper stuffed in the floor cracks didn't stop their draft. The days of summer seemed years away, yet somehow I thought of grasshoppers and crickets. I recalled a spiteful story I'd heard from lantern-faced Norbert Pfeifer, who in Salzburg had stuck out his tongue at me. Now our neighbor in the next partition, he'd told me about an unhappy one-legged soldier trying to adjust. A grasshopper missing one of its hind legs crawled across a tablecloth toward that cripple's glass. The unhappy soldier's friend pointed out the grasshopper and the manly way it hobbled. "Courage," he said, and the cripple's face relaxed. And then the grasshopper took off on two good wings.

"What are you waiting for?" said Franz and Ludwig.

"This isn't America," added Franz. "Get serious, kid."

I must have looked puzzled.

"They're not players like the Russians," said Ludwig, as if to gauge my reaction.

That gave me pause. I wanted Americans to be playing. Just the same, I hid a white and black pawn in my two fists, for Ludwig to choose who'd open.

He chuckled. "You open, kid. I'll give you that."

I'd be dead regardless. I was going to lose badly. But in the back of my mind, somehow, I thought I had to begin somewhere to become a champion. That evening, it occurred to me, Father as always would send me out for fresh bread at Frau Hollinger's, the same fragrant rye from which the two cripples had kneaded their spare knights. So at first I positioned my two knights, for luck. They could jump, if not fly. Whatever Franz and Ludwig had, I liked my odds. Win, lose, or draw, I couldn't lose.

CHAPTER 9

DOWN UNDER

A few weeks after our epic match—Ludwig had crushed me—the snows began to melt. A raw wind swept down the foothills. Reading in our partition, I pulled the horse blanket around me. On the other side of our thin wall, with great earnestness, I heard little Milan Boban's mother say, "*Brtati.*" At least that's how it sounded. From her footsteps in the corridor, I guessed she had just returned from cleaning rooms at the inn, Zum Hirschen; it stood by the south bridge, where Herr Gruber eventually lived. Like everyone, she tried to make ends meet.

That "brtati" warmed me up; I doubled up in silent laughter. In the camp we all found ways to get our digs in. Milan was a denizen of classroom 2a. I heard him shuffle, I think embarrassed, as he denied her charge. When she again accused him of farting, Milan caved.

"It's the bean soup. I can't help it," he yammered in Croatian.

"Next time, go outside!" said Dubravka Boban. "We're not living in a sty."

Lying on my bunk bed reading on the other side—I read anything I could get my hands on, school lessons, newsprint scraps from the camp latrine, even catalogs from the American army dump—I cleared my throat. I wanted Milan to know someone listened. He liked to cause trouble; he should know someone was on to him. Even our neighbor on the other side, Norbert Pfeifer, hated him, and not because he was Croatian. Milan was a stoolie and a precocious lecher. Pug-nosed and beetle-browed, he looked more Serb than Croatian. But if the beans embarrassed him, lucky for him his mother didn't know the latest.

The next morning his eyes looked dark with secret sorrow. Leaving for school, I heard his steps behind me at the barracks door. He tried to scamper past me.

I looked past him. "*Brtati!*"

Milan trotted past the camp latrine by the riverbank and looked over his shoulder. "*Svinjo jedno!*"

I caught up to him. "You're the pig!"

"Who's been teaching you Croatian?" he said, sullen.

"Our neighbors," I said. "Every word, every fart."

Of course those neighbors were his family. The Salzach River rushed beside us, swollen with spring runoff. The road was barely flecked with snow, but the foothills and peaks around us still kept their winter coat. Snowdrops and crocuses bloomed in the wet soil along the road. The somber Milan trudged on.

"Be careful, or I'll tell your father about Ponkratz and his bloody nose."

How did Milan know? Word was getting out; that wasn't good.

"You do that," I said, shutting him up, "and someone may just mention your spying. You think people in this miserable camp want to be exposed, like that? Take old Baumann, for example. Friend of your father's, isn't he?"

Milan's mouth dropped shut. He hurried ahead to escape me. The latrine now lay behind us, the site of his latest misdeeds. By the time I crossed the north bridge into town, sprinkled below the picture-postcard Alps, he trotted far ahead. His bag bounced on his back. I hoped I'd shut him up for good, still relieved Fräulein Seebach hadn't talked to Father.

Berti Krummbacher was behind this, I was sure. He'd told Norbert Pfeifer, who then passed word to Milan. My tripping Gustl Ponkratz was a real lesson; I wasn't usually that careless. But when Gustl had shown off that juicy bun with meat, it was the last straw. Our classmates all disliked him, probably even his poor cousins Naz and Poldi. No sense to rub it in. Everyone was dirt-poor. It wasn't just us refugees.

But without any help from me, fate soon cornered Milan.

Norbert Pfeifer told me he'd been spying around the camp latrine. Milan sought out what was seedy. Like Franz and Ludwig, he and his gang already favored female parts, which consumed their feverish thoughts. The camp latrine stood just across the graveled road between our leaky barracks and the Salzach River. An oblong wooden box, it held a door and three wooden seats worn smooth. The box looked innocent but was cantilevered over the riverbank. The seats were placed so as to drop their cargo directly into its muddy flow, to be swept downstream toward the city of Mozart. But users didn't know that sitting down they bared their behinds to Milan's gang, ogling from the bank below.

One day Stipe Baumann happened to look through his toilet seat before he sat and glimpsed them snickering. He recognized Milan's face.

"*Kurva banda!*" raged old Baumann, hitching up his pants.

That evening he reported to Franjo Boban, Milan's father. I heard it piping hot from Norbert. His granny was friends with Baumann's wife, old Katica. Norbert's face mocked her disgust, but his voice already relished what he thought would follow. His tale helped explain the later uproar in the Boban partition.

That evening, as soon as Milan's father returned from work, he sounded like an unchained bear. German only in name, Baumann must have spoken to him as a fellow Croatian.

"*Nemoj battine,*" little Milan began his lament, or so it sounded. "Don't hit me!"

"*Udriga!*" spat his mother, refusing to protect him. "Let him have it," she urged Franjo. "For all I know, I could have sat in place of Stipe. My bum visible to all!"

In our partition, Father looked at me sternly. "Know anything about this, Konrad?"

I looked at the Bobans' wall. "Nothing."

"Whatever he's due, he probably deserved it."

"Shouldn't you step in? Franjo's about to kill him," Mother said.

"He'll stop short," said Father. "The little shit's his pride and joy. What would be the point, with the whole clan about to head for Australia?"

It was the first I'd heard of the Bobans leaving, for Australia no less. It rated higher than Colombia or anywhere in South America, and apparently it had tons of Croats. I asked, "When are they going?"

I should have kept my mouth shut. Father gave me his full attention.

"Remember, you're a Kemper. It's your job to keep your nose clean. This camp's lousy with indignities; I don't want you to contribute."

Just then Herr Gruber returned, his cheeks flushed, smiling genially. I was grateful he'd entered but also that he'd just missed Father's gruff words. Although lately I didn't see him much, in some way we were still friends. Even then I think I realized the camp could have warped me beyond repair without Father to tug my reins. My nose wasn't exactly clean, not with tripping Gustl Ponkratz and other deeds or omissions that hadn't yet borne fruit. It wasn't smart just now for me to test Father's limits.

As the tumult next door subsided, Milan still whimpered. I could almost imagine his pug nose through the partition, sniffling at his beating but even more at the loss of his father's favor. I felt almost sorry for him.

I changed my mind over the next few days as I began to realize fully they were destined for the land down under. But again fate intervened when we all saw a vision of America. It happened in the school basement, like our charity lunches of polenta and other good things, though Father liked to joke that "good things usually come from above."

I'd just finished with shots for whooping cough and gotten back to school. The doctor's needle was the biggest I'd ever seen, and he wielded it with relish. It almost took my breath away, whatever I had left from coughing. I thought briefly of Ludwig's penciled cheeks, but mine were real and hurt. I recovered just in time for Mother to start wheezing. As she expelled hot gobs of phlegm, her breath whistled. And then, just a few days later, our special lesson took my mind off it.

It was a treat. Fräulein Seebach led us downstairs to the cafeteria with its quaint prints of Austrian girls in peasant costumes. Its benches had been aligned to face a screen. It flickered with an animated film made in America, showing a bouncy little man on board a ship throwing a drowning man a life preserver. The two cartoon figures were lean and linear, not plumped up like Ludwig's cheeks. Other classes joined us for the film, and even Poldi and Naz seemed to focus. They wore their patched sweaters, although Naz glared at me. Once the film started, though, his eyes were nailed to the screen; his comrade Poldi stashed his pocket knife, his other hand still kneading the plug of wood he'd whittled. Just the same, I sat with Herbert Mautner between them and me.

Fräulein Seebach would probably say more later—that somehow the film was important. For now she briefly explained what it meant, including the block letters on the life preserver—ERP—and how America would help us and Europe. "European Recovery Program," she said momentously. "The Marshall Plan."

Australia paled beside this.

Back in our classroom she got out her methodical atlas to help illustrate this development. Although it showed the European borders from 1903, her finger traced a line from north to south through Germany and what had been Austria-Hungary.

"It's the Iron Curtain, children," she said ruefully. To the east sprawled Russia, now the Soviet Union, huge and squeezing the West. "The war crushed us completely. The Marshall Plan," she said, "will help us rebuild and resist the East."

I could almost imagine Western Europe strain, a weak collection of islands and peninsulas—a mere appendage to the land mass to the east. Before I got too carried away, Herbert Mautner said coolly, "My father thinks otherwise."

"How is that, Herbert?" Fräulein Seebach asked gently.

Herbert glanced at me. "If America had won the peace in 1919," he said, "the second war wouldn't have happened."

She seemed pained. "A good point, Herbert. But the war did happen. And now, children, we need what help we can get."

CHAPTER 10

PROSPECTING

As though the cartoon had prepared me, I began to look out for America. Even years later, I'd continue my discoveries—among them, discovering what I'd eaten.

America was a far cry from Milan Boban or even Herbert and his buried men. That first spring in Straubling was full of promise and discovery. Berti, the switchman's son, as usual sounded the alarm. From their little yellow house on the embankment of the railroad tracks, he had an open view toward the dump ground off the riverbank. He could spot the army truck pull up before any of us, something he never allowed us to forget. Still, we all ran.

Father would laugh. "It's in their blood. Switchmen, even Berti, learn perfect timing early." He talked as if he knew Berti and old Fritz Krummbacher better than anyone. I had no idea one day we'd be neighbors.

"Disgusting," said Mother. It had become her word for all occasions.

"Can't be helped," said Father. "Whatever you seek and find, just don't fall off the edge of the known world from joy," he told me. He didn't entirely approve of my exertions, but he knew boys needed outlets. And sometimes I'd find him pencils he couldn't otherwise afford. Once even a rusty hammer!

"Do you have to encourage him?" Mother scolded. "At least wash up," she'd tell me afterward. "Who knows what rot you'll contract?"

After our recent whooping coughs, her advice was worth considering.

Again Father laughed. "Just remember, Konrad, you're destined to discover America."

"They're unloading!" Berti sounded his alarm downstream.

Even from a distance, we could all see the olive truck against the snow-capped Alps. As it disgorged its load off the riverbank we ran toward the nearby north bridge. As Berti jostled me I almost ran him down. I decided my nose could outdo his and let him trot ahead. A little dignity couldn't hurt. Father was right—never seem too eager. I'd find whatever I found, and whatever I did, probably more interesting than Berti's. He lacked imagination. Behind us a forgettable clan edged closer—Milan, little Jiři Kratky, and more camp boys, with a wheezing Norbert bringing up the rear.

Soon we clumped across the wooden bridge toward the dump ground off the Salzach River. Near the other side of the bridge a creek disgorged another offering—entrails and cattle tripe from Anton Ponkratz's butcher shop, that of Gustl's father. Having washed down the embankment, they billowed in an eddy where the creek struck river water. Before we even reached the dump ground, the army truck had rumbled off. Today's mound, I saw right off, looked rich and worth exploring.

Tall and superior, a conqueror of his realm, Berti stood over the puffing Norbert and the rest of us who picked. But soon even he succumbed to prospecting. The take was bountiful, though not without its smells and rude coagulations. I stumbled over bags of wet black soil, coffee grounds, as I learned. They must have come from the garrison mess hall, and I threw them back, disgusted. I wasn't interested in the slices of spongy white bread, either, in bags of cellophane. Frau Hollinger's crunchy rye was far superior. Suddenly I nearly slid down to the river and recalled Father's words.

As I stumbled over rolls of soft white tissue, bags of cracked shells broke my fall; they mixed almond shells and chips of brazil nuts, which the soldiers apparently called "nigger toes." But the cellophane bags often included unshelled nuts that we could crack and eat. Berti found a broken fountain pen to repair and sell. As we treaded, cigarette butts worked their way out of pockets of ash. Then I made a real find, a spoon marked USN. Mother would be overjoyed. Norbert looked at me greedily, as if pleading with me to let him have it for his granny. Soon I found something new, packets of cards with festive lettering and notes in red or blue. The cards pictured a spotless world—green wreaths on red doors, a blue house against clean snow, children racing sleds down slopes with dark green firs, and a red barn from which a horse pulled out a sleigh with bells.

Berti sneered before I could puzzle them out. "They're just American Christmas cards."

I lunged toward him but he already had another find. The torn catalog was crammed with pictures of tools, furniture, boxed fruit, and dizzying arrays of shirts, shoes, dresses, striped candies, and more. Berti snickered over young women whose limbs swelled from lacy underwear. I looked and shrugged. Franz and Ludwig might have stared, having lovingly drawn those cheeks.

"The disgusting little runt," I could already hear Mother say.

And I heard Father laugh. "A future switchman, keeping his eyes peeled."

"The things children learn in this camp."

"A useful reference," Father said. He had a knack for mystery.

Now I spied something important. It was one of those booklets they called "comics," which Father disdained. Unlike the Marshall Plan cartoon, its drawings were in little frames with balloons of words. The booklet's stained cover said, *The Master of Ballantrae.* Even though I couldn't read the English texts, the silent pictures haunted me. In an upper corner of the cover, in black letters in a yellow box, appeared the words *Classics Illustrated*, and the booklet smelled of ink and fragrant telltale pulp.

I stuffed it quickly inside my shirt so neither Berti or Norbert could see it. Looking up from the water's edge, little Jiři Kratky seemed to glimpse it but was too small to count although he'd escaped his mother. I held one arm over my shirt. By our oil lamp that evening or above the camp in Palfner's fields, I would pore over its drawings fueled with haunting mystery. They were even better than playing chess. Someday I'd learn the English words. In fact, of all the refugees only Father, seeing possibilities of which most of us hadn't dared to dream, had begun to study English under one of the parish priests. Klaus Sekyra's lessons were to help him get ready for America.

Suddenly a stranger motioned to me, likely a former soldier, not a refugee. Absorbed in my discoveries, I didn't notice him until late. Adults didn't usually join us boys; it was beneath their dignity. His face looked like dried-out jerky, some of which I'd found the week before. It wasn't just his bony face. A Wehrmacht coat dangled around his thin shoulders, its insignia torn off. He made me think of Ludwig—the same ferocity when he hissed, "Hey, kid, take a look."

I didn't like his tone. He held up a nubbly object like a thick dark thumb. My mouth must have hung open. Beneath its crust of dirt, I just might find chocolate.

His jutting cheekbones made him look like a wolf. "I'll make you a deal," he almost snarled.

"What kind of a deal?" I said. You couldn't trust adults, except maybe Father.

"I'll trade you this," he said, "for any cigarette butts you find." He must not have found too many.

I kept my presence of mind. "Give it to me first."

"Here. But cheat on me, and I'll have your liver for breakfast."

I snatched the object from him, trembling, and sniffed it like a cigar. Pay dirt. A chocolate bar without a wrapper, but real chocolate and still good. Fifteen minutes later I handed him a cache of cigarette butts, just as I'd once gathered them for Herr Gruber. He poured them in a pocket of his grimy coat.

"Until next time," he grunted and clambered up the mound.

He must have lusted for a smoke but didn't want to show he was desperate. Due to his size and impatience, he dislodged some of the dump ground as he climbed. Christmas cards, toilet paper, and kitchen garbage tumbled down toward me. I slid toward the Salzach River but near the water's edge grabbed a willow branch.

"Who was that fool?" Berti sneered out of his hearing. "He almost touched off an avalanche."

"How would I know? Probably just passing through."

"More likely scum from Eastern Europe."

I touched my shirt to hear the crinkling paper of *The Master of Ballantrae,* then felt my pocket to confirm the chocolate bar. "Some of this load of shit," I said, trying out Father's most acerbic tone, "deserves to be swept away." I clambered up the mound toward the horizon of the Alps. "And that goes for you too."

Berti raised his grimy fist. "Balkan trash!"

"I speak better German than you."

"Go back to where you came from."

That evening, back from his new job as a construction helper, Father caught me reading *The Master of Ballantrae.* Or rather devouring the pictures, an act he somehow found offensive. The shifting light of our petroleum lamp made the shadowy drawings dance.

"If we ever get to America," he said, "I expect you to use your opportunities. To do that, you'll need to read. Pictures alone won't do it. And before you can ever read in English, you'll have to read more, period."

"I want to," I said. "But I need things to read." I had in mind adventure books.

"Your schoolbooks come first. The rest will take care of itself."

I never missed homework, if not for him, then for Fräulein Seebach. But *The Master* had whetted my appetite. "Teach me to read English," I said eagerly.

Father weighed my enthusiasm. "I'm just starting to learn," he admitted. "I don't want to teach you my beginner's mistakes. For now just study the words—gauge their feel and weight. Even that picture rag will let you do that. English is different from German, but many words are similar. Look beyond the pictures. Once you're in school in America, you'll have no trouble." He seemed to see an opportunity. "Americans read too many comic books. That opens the door for immigrants."

He sounded dismissive, but it was the first time he made me think we might actually get to America. I could feel my heart leap. Then he conceded, "This picture book's good for starters. Where did you find it?"

"The American dump ground."

"Be careful in it. Who else was there?"

"The whole gang. Norbert, Milan Boban, and the rest. All the boys run when they hear the shout!" I didn't mention my bargain with the stranger scrounging for cigarettes.

"Whose shout?"

"Berti Krummbacher."

Father snorted. "There's no dignity in running. But we're favored by the gods."

"What do you mean?"

I'd almost forgotten *The Master*. Father had a knack for mystery, and I wanted more of his news of America. Although a farmer back home, he was a born teacher.

"Be glad we're in the American zone," added Father, chuckling. "If we lived under the Soviets all you'd find is vodka bottles. Empty ones, you can be sure."

"And maybe a moldy potato," Mother broke in, heating our soup ration on our makeshift stove.

Before Father sent me out for bread, I turned back to *The Master of Ballantrae*. The taste of the chocolate bar still sang in my mouth. That afternoon, after climbing up into the hills, I'd brushed off the dirt, finding the expected bite marks. I passed the bar under my nose, inhaling its scent, the way Father had told me some men did with cigars. It was rich with silken chocolate, nubbly peanuts, blond caramel, and a central chewy core, a mother lode of something even more precious than its chocolate coat. Years later, in America, I found out it was nougat. As I studied its white wrapper with red and blue lettering, I learned the name of this miniature paradise. It turned out to be a Baby Ruth.

In the meantime the *Classics Illustrated* crackled in my shirt as I lay in Palfner's meadow overlooking our barracks by the riverside. Spring was full of promise. I would get to the *Classics* soon, but not just yet. It was always good to hold something in reserve. Puffy clouds rose into the sky above me far beyond the Alps. I raised the chocolate to my mouth and sank my teeth into the bar. Life was good.

CHAPTER 11

A REUNION

By then I rarely saw the emperor. He still shared our tiny partition, but mostly he just slept there. I didn't find out why until later. During the day I hardly saw him. But that spring Herr Gruber got some news from the Red Cross. His daughter, Erna, had been found.

They'd lost each other in 1945 on their refugee trek out of Czech territory. She apparently hid on a farm near the restored border with Austria. After working there a few years she managed to flee to Austria and entered a refugee camp near Linz. Like Herr Gruber she started a search with the Red Cross. In her camp, in the meantime, she met a young German from Odessa. Now they roomed in Linz over a bakery, and Ivan Zimmermann had found work as a chemist.

Herr Gruber held her letter, forwarded by the Red Cross. As he sat on his bunk his fingers trembled around it; his hand had age spots like splotches. His peasant coat with green piping hung on a nail above him. From repeated readings his daughter's letter had wrinkled, but I could tell Mother was excited. If things worked out, the emperor might be leaving us. We lived cramped and crowded, as even Father had to admit.

"What wonderful news," she said.

The emperor's handlebars quivered. "I'm overwhelmed. I'd given up hope."

"You'll want to see her soon, I'm sure."

"As a matter of fact, I'm taking the train to Linz tomorrow. I'll try not to wake you." Herr Gruber eagerly spoke of spending his "last days with the children."

"We have friends near Linz too," Father said.

"Actually, in nearby Wels," corrected Mother.

"A young couple from our hometown," Father said. "The Marschalls, just itching to emigrate. I don't know how they got out of Yugoslavia in time. They've found work at an American base; Stefan's helping out in the kitchen. You might say they're primed. If any of us find a way to reach America, I'm sure they'll be the first."

"A kitchen's always a good start. They haven't written in a while," Mother said. She thought they put on airs.

"We'll see you off," Father told Herr Gruber. "It's the least we can do."

"Please, my friends, no," said the emperor. "It's absurdly unnecessary. After everything you've done for me—and at such an early hour."

Father winked at me. "Nonsense. It'll start your day right."

As he got ready the next morning the emperor's eyes twinkled. The handlebar mustache was superb, and someone had pressed his suit. It was Mother's turn to wink: a special lady friend. Father had lit our petroleum lamp. I still don't know how Mother managed it, but she had a snack for the emperor. On the way out we heard Franz curse in the invalids' partition, and someone rustled nearby, probably Granny Pfeifer.

Father and I walked Herr Gruber to the station, just now dark and silent—the same station where we'd tumbled to Straubling's tracks. It lay upstream on our side of the murmuring Salzach, and after we said goodbye I continued on to school.

The emperor returned Sunday, just two days later.

"Yes," he said only. "Yes, Herr Kemper, yes."

It was all he seemed able to say. Father made consoling sounds. Herr Gruber didn't stay for our usual ration of black bean soup. Sitting before the barracks that Sunday afternoon he spoke haltingly with Father as Franz and Ludwig hobbled past, then left for the inn, Zum Hirschen. Late that night he staggered back and woke us. But Father had been awake and helped him into bed. The next morning Herr Gruber looked gray and his mustache drooped. He did go to work to split kindling wood at Greiff's, a local merchant.

Something was wrong and serious. I liked the emperor. Maybe he reminded me of Grandfather Wendt. In a way we'd always be friends, despite school and my many projects. "What's the matter with Herr Gruber?" I asked Father when I had a chance.

Father explained that the emperor's daughter had been distant. "But not a word to anyone." It seemed Erna and her new husband, Ivan Zimmermann, had discouraged Herr Gruber. They wanted to get ahead and felt it wasn't wise for him to join them. Anyway, their two-room walk-up was tiny. And apparently Herr Gruber had liked a drink or two even before the war.

Father said the war had softened some and hardened others. "With all they must have gone through," he scoffed, "you'd think his only daughter and this Ivan would show more feeling."

His words coincided with the rumblings between him and Mother during the emperor's short absence. Little by little I pieced the truth out. It had to do with Father's earlier promise that Herr Gruber's stay with us would be temporary. Although Father didn't yet know where we'd land, he had a preference. But no matter where, he felt, in the refugee camp we'd be just as temporary as the emperor. Yet Mother—despite the crowded camp, the noisy children, the gossip and indignities, the camp's supervisor Gustav Finger and his toady, Spitz, despite all this and everything, our being second class in Austria, and her extra work for Herr Gruber—clung to Europe.

"Sooner or later," threatened Father.

Mother was aghast.

"We're going to America."

"I don't want to go."

She said it whenever she wanted the last word. It was her phrase for settling all arguments. Father saw this as obstinacy, not a real objection to America. She wanted to be consulted. She didn't like change anyway, even change for the better, as if to protest Father's bargain with Herr Gruber, which I think she felt had been hasty. She could be contrary anyway, unless there was good reason to accept Father's view or she gained some benefit. Her small resentment could be dangerous, and Father's mellow humor aroused her more.

Now there was Herr Gruber's misery. She felt sorry for him, but he seemed to feed her resentment.

In the meantime Straubling had no public gardens for collecting cigarette stubs for the emperor. Instead I struck bargains with the devil like the stranger at the dump ground. School and so on occupied me. More refugees found work in construction, as helpers, or still shoveled snow off railroad tracks. Even Herr Gruber had begun to find odd jobs with shopkeepers, like the grain merchant Greiff, running errands or splitting kindling wood. Even before he went to see his daughter, he filled his pipe with cheap store-bought tobacco instead of scavenging cigarette butts and began to stop in town for beer. As Father told it, he would have a glass or two in the evenings and more on weekends, his habit long before the war. Mother sometimes complained that his pipe smoke got deep into our clothes and sheets, and she smelled beer on his breath. Then Father would mention America, and she didn't want to go.

"Nonsense," repeated Father.

Surprisingly, one morning after Herr Gruber's return from Linz, before I left for school and Father and Mother left for work, she said invincibly, "What about America?"

Father didn't seem surprised, as if he'd watched the shift build inside her.

"I thought you might change your mind," he said with a trace of melancholy. "I'll go to Salzburg to see what I can start, even if not to America."

Mother could be tough when you least expected it. "What do you mean? I thought you said America."

"They won't take just anyone."

"It's America or nothing."

Father chose to laugh. "My thinking exactly. Listen to me, Anni. Have you ever, even once, known me to plan anything I didn't think was best for us?"

"Ha!" But instead of being angry at not being consulted, she suddenly added, "So you thought that, did you?"

"What's that?"

"You thought I'd change my mind."

Father flung out his thick hands and rolled his eyes toward heaven.

Herr Gruber, in the meantime, whenever he had a little money, now spent almost every evening at his inn, Zum Hirschen. For three weeks we hardly saw him except when he stumbled into our partition. Franjo Boban cursed next door about these late arrivals although he wouldn't confront Father. Herr Gruber wasn't really sober even when he went to work. Mother became increasingly short with all of us and made Father just as irritable, but he still felt sorry for the emperor. They no longer exchanged old army tales. Mother began to support our American cause with fervor. Almost daily she would ask Father about some detail or other, desirable places to settle or the status of our papers, even though as yet Father had nothing specific to report. Canada and Australia were easier options, but increasingly Mother insisted on America. There was a hitch, I found out later, but Father seemed content to hold out for her. Without realizing it, she'd backed into what he secretly wanted. He'd won her over to America.

Not that they were idealists. Father saw the New World as a grand opportunity—and more for me than anyone. Mother saw a chance to escape the refugee camp and now the emperor. She couldn't be blamed, of course, even though Herr Gruber gave her money for his laundry. One night the drunken emperor soiled his bunk bed. In the morning, Mother put her foot down.

Her eyes bored into Father's. "What about America?"

Father agreed things had become intolerable. Mother didn't have the will to tell Herr Gruber, but Father quietly spoke to him. To this day I wonder what he told the emperor. Fortunately Austria had started giving a little money to elderly refugees. Herr Gruber announced he would take a room at his regular inn, Zum Hirschen. It was an awkward moment.

"Dear friends, I've been a burden. How can I ever repay you?"

I realized I'd miss him; he'd always treated me with kindly courtesy.

"It was nothing, Herr Gruber," said Father, courtly, still using the formal address for someone older. "For now we're all refugees, gnawing on the same bone. It's a soup the war cooked up, and we have to ladle it together."

Herr Gruber had almost nothing to move out except his coat, his pipe, and knotty cane. "Black bean soup at that," he managed. "With hardly a meat bone in it."

That broke the ice. Mother and Father laughed. I opened our partition door for him just in time to glimpse little Jiři Kratky peeking up at me, his eyes like shiny black buttons. Blond Hedwig Hutz spied with him. They ran off. The emperor took his coat off its nail, added his pipe and burnished cane, and that was that.

Only not quite. Remembering our goodbye to Grandfather as the partition door closed behind him, Mother suddenly began to sob. Then she went uptown to work as always, cleaning and scrubbing floors.

CHAPTER 12

SOLDIER'S GIRL

Margit Massong had bright red lips, the kind you got from eating ripe raspberries. Only I doubted that, since it was too early in the summer. And only if some boyfriend fetched her the berries. She had pretensions. You had to be humble to stoop for raspberries by the creek, and preferably small, since it flowed through Palfner's meadow. Margit fit what the locals called an *Ami Flitschn*, a floozy girlfriend of American soldiers. It was one of few opinions our camp and the locals shared. She sought a shortcut to America. And while a refugee like the rest of us, she looked down her nose at us.

I guessed some Yanks found her attractive, but I couldn't see why. She had fierce, long-lashed eyes, but she lacked the plump flesh Ludwig lavished on his sketched behinds. Still, once I saw him stare at her—she ignored him—and late one Saturday with the crickets chirping, I saw her clasped in American arms. I'd stepped behind the barracks to avoid the camp latrine. He was a Yankee from the garrison on the opposite riverbank, I barely saw in that dim light. His brows were thick like little Milan's, his hair blond, and he wore a smart dress uniform darkened by the shadows. On its thick green cloth I saw brass buttons glint.

Margit sounded high-strung: "Get lost."

The easy-going soldier added something. It was humiliating not to know those scraps of English. The two left intertwined.

In the morning Mother said the floozy's boyfriend hailed from a small town—it sounded like Barberton—in the central state of Ohio. Mother still mourned Grandfather but she couldn't ignore this juicy story. She always had that romantic if gossipy side, buried but tenacious. Boyfriends were romantic, especially in a camp like ours. Apparently a decent fellow, he'd walk Margit home from dancing and even promised they would marry. Mother had it directly from the floozy's mother, Nanschi Massong.

"For her sake, I hope so," she told Father. "It's probably her last chance."

"Women," Father said.

It was a dangerous thing to say. "What do you know about women, Hans?"

"Why can't they treat each other nicely?"

She mentioned some of the camp's slimier males. "What about Gustav Finger and Toni Spitz?"

"Of course," conceded Father. "I only meant more generosity."

"It's this camp, as you said. It's being widowed, with children and no fathers. Just take Kratky, for example."

Now they agreed. "Exactly, a dragon," Father said, glad to drop the subject.

Vera Kratky was a refugee from Bohemia with a brood of hungry little ones, including button-eyed Jiři. She had arms like tree trunks yet with her brood seemed forever one arm short. With her pulled-back hair and eyes like slots, she didn't look like a German from the Sudetenland, and despite her last name she wasn't short.

As if to prove Father's point, that Sunday afternoon Kratky and Wilma Hutz put on a show, a nasty eruption of their simmering feud. Despite little Jiři and blond Hedwig, their offspring and playmates, they disagreed no matter what. It was hard to miss the eruption at our barracks entrance, opposite the stripped carcass of a Wehrmacht truck down by the riverbank. I listened from the hallway just to keep my hand in. You never knew when something might turn out to be useful. Mother saw me and asked what I was up to.

I put my finger to my lips. "They're at it again."

"Shame on you." She shooed me off.

Today's pretext for the two women was Margit Massong. I left for Mother's sake, then sneaked right back.

"At least it's a step up," spat Vera Kratky, "from waiting at the garrison gate on pay days with the local bitches." She looked like Genghis Khan.

"For their American heroes with bulging pants, and not just money wads. Let's just see if it lasts."

I almost felt sorry for the floozy. I couldn't spot her mother anywhere. Nanschi would have jumped right in, but maybe she'd gone uptown. Other refugees now gathered, giving Kratky her audience.

"Somebody should rescue that boy from her clutches," sniped Wilma Hutz, a rail-thin blonde with pinched blue eyes and those two daughters, Hedwig and Gerda.

It was rumored she flirted with our camp shepherd, the Reverend Simon Dachnagl. Once she'd thrown scalding broth over Toni Spitz, the cook, when he slurred about it in the soup line. Before I could visualize Dachnagl on his spiritual rounds, their words grew more shrill.

"You should talk," hissed Kratky.

"Just what do you mean?" said Hutz.

Kratky pinched her thumb and index finger together in Hutz's face. Margit had been a pretext. "There's more space between these fingers than between you and that hussy. What a way to teach our kids."

Wilma's fingers leaped to Kratky's eyes. Vera twisted the blonde braids Hutz had piled atop her head. From their screams it was hard to tell who got the best of it.

"Bohemian sow. You don't even look German!"

"*Kanaille!*" raged Kratky. Between the legs of the gathered crowd I saw her little Jiři, his eyes those black buttons.

I felt Granny Pfeifer snuffle behind me, taking it in. A traffic jam had built and even her grandson, Norbert, had joined us. He'd apparently run in from the distant kitchen. Had he sneaked something to eat? Now dried-up Stipe Baumann, the Croat in all but name, craned his head.

His wife Katica yanked him back. "*Magarac!*"

"Leave me be," he snapped.

"Jackass," she repeated, "you're worse than an old woman."

The two invalids, Franz and Ludwig, hobbled from their partition by the entrance, interrupted at chess. Franz cursed under his breath while Ludwig braced one arm against the doorway and brandished a crutch with the other.

"Quiet," he growled. "How can we do justice to the sport of kings?"

For a minute I forgave Ludwig his merciless earlier victory, the way he'd ground me down. I still wanted a rematch—but with the spiteful Franz. Luckily Father wasn't in the crowd. He would have sent me packing more quickly than Mother. Still, at Ludwig's words the two women stopped short. Somehow the two gritty invalids made everyone keep their distance. Kratky and Hutz withdrew.

And just in time, because now Margit's mother joined in. She must have just gotten back, or she would have joined the fight right off. Nanschi Massong was no one to trifle with. It was obvious to whom Margit owed her dark burning eyes.

"What's going on?" she groused suspiciously, finding Mother.

Mother tried to calm her. "A silly spat among the women, about nothing."

"In this lousy camp, nothing's nothing."

Mother invited her back inside. "Forget it, Nanschi. Tell me more about your daughter's good fortune."

"About time, too, for something to go the kid's way."

"I hear he's from Ohio. There's lots of Germans there."

"There's a Berlin, and a Steubenville, and who knows what else?" said Nanschi, seeming well-informed. "Margit's young man knows only a little German, but yesterday he brought a map. We may have relatives in Barberton! Distant but American, even if they fixed their names. There's Slovenes too, and even Greeks and Croats."

"What's the young man's name?" asked Mother.

It sounded like Granić, Matt Granić. With that name, for all I knew, he could have been pug-nosed Milan's cousin. "America's a real melting pot," Nanschi bubbled, "just like our old Austria-Hungary."

Father would have liked this conversation. He must have been helping his friend Florian Riedl with something, or he would have been here. He liked to think Austria-Hungary was the original melting pot. Sometimes he pondered the fate of the millions of Germans scattered throughout Eastern Europe, especially Austria-Hungary, long before the war. For centuries they'd settled in places like Poland, Romania, and as far away as the Volga, not just in Hungary or the later Yugoslavia or Herr Gruber's Sudetenland. For Father, after the war these ancient German settlements had formed an avalanche of misery and hopes, a stew of millions displaced toward Austria and Germany and then worldwide. Like so many, they sought to escape Communism to start new lives elsewhere.

Almost as quickly, I realized that listening to Nanschi he might have gone into one of his black moods about these displaced millions—including Kratky, Wilma Hutz, the emperor, and countless others like us, even scum like Gustav Finger and Toni Spitz. Nanschi Massong had too much spirit to dwell on such thoughts, although what she said sounded true. Most of us from central Europe and the Balkans had our roots in Austria-Hungary, whether Hungarian, German, Croatian or Bohemian, even the sprinkling of French descendants from Lorraine. Nanschi herself looked more French than anything and proudly traced her roots to a Paul Masson, an eighteenth century French-speaking carpenter. Now her daughter might just marry a Croat from Ohio.

"Just you wait long enough," she said with a laugh, "and everything comes full circle."

As if in answer, we heard the trooping soldiers.

CHAPTER 13

GUM AND CHOCOLATES

The unfortunate Yanks were out training on a Sunday. They jogged toward us in cadence on the way north to Lechner's bottomland. Set between the gravel road and a bend in the Salzach River, his lush stretch flooded periodically. It made Alois Lechner heartsick to watch the troops and jeeps tear up his land just as he tried to nurse it back. There was no winning, he'd tell Father. During the war, under the rain and snow, it had served as a camp for Soviet POWs. Even now he'd find rusty spoons or moldering rags torn from the soil by the Yankee maneuvers. I knew the land. Once Berti Krummbacher and I had gone to reconnoiter the terrain, finding brass casings, ruts, gashes, and muddy Coca-Cola bottles. But that's another story.

The troops' cadence brought me back. The Americans were young and tall, unlike us scrawny refugees or the stocky local boys, and they loped rhythmically in laced boots and floppy uniforms they called "fatigues." Some of the soldiers were dark and olive-skinned, whom Father called *Spagnoler*—his word for Spaniards. As the chanting got closer our camp scavengers descended, drowning out their chant. Norbert Pfeifer and Milan's gang included Jiři, Hedwig, and more snot-nosed Kratkys. They had learned to plead, "Gum, gum," but even more they begged for "Chocolate!"

Laughing soldiers threw out small Hershey bars, and the children lunged.

In the soldiers' wake, in fact, goods and cash blossomed everywhere. Mother, for example, itched to take in soldiers' laundry. It paid much better than scrubbing floors at Stubaier's or cleaning for Dr. Deutlinger, a dentist who'd fled Vienna's Soviet zone. She began urging Father to find us another place, however humble, so she could have a laundry shed. It wasn't just to help feed us; I think it was a secret ambition to earn more money doing laundry than Father earned at construction sites.

Throughout Straubling the American garrison boosted trade. There was the dump ground off the riverbank whose benefits I already knew. A chocolate bar, a *Classics Illustrated*, sometimes pencils, even thick bottles of wine-red Coca-Cola or that muddy spoon marked USN. A local builder, Taxenbacher, put up housing for the troops and officers' families, and raised the concrete pylons with barbed wire around their compound that kept the locals out. His profits and wages helped feed his workers and local shops. Stubaier's inn, Zum Karpfen, began doing a roaring business. He might vent at drunken American soldiers flirting with local women or defiling his premises with their Ami Flitschn, but he suffered gladly. Business was business. I had it all on Father's word.

Even if some of the *Amis* staggered out of Stubaier's singing and disorderly, he served them without a murmur. With his cronies he even found time to stare at black soldiers. It piqued his curiosity to hear the old-timers' latest theory on why some randy Flitschn would think black soldiers might be more potent.

On rare nights out with Mother, all Father would say was, "Nonsense."

As he told it, his friend Florian Riedl, the lumberjack, chuckled over his beer while his girlfriend grimaced. Florian always had his unique perspective. He probably would have had the same on my latest hero, the American boxer Jersey Joe Walcott.

"They're built like trucks. I bet they'd make fine lumberjacks."

"*Primitives* is the word," a tipsy Toni Spitz had opined at a nearby table. Our camp cook's nose was everywhere, and drinking made him more obnoxious. "Noble savages," he sang, digging himself in deeper. His wife Ilon tried to hush him. "Nothing doing, I'll speak my mind."

Father ignored him. The three black soldiers at a corner table enjoyed their foaming pilsner.

"It's a good thing they don't know German," said Florian.

"They'd crush him like a slug," said Father.

Spitz crowed more insults, with Ilon in pain. Father never told me what he finally said to Spitz to shut him up.

Now the floozy entered with her American soldier, Matt Granić. They did a slow dance. Then she began to teach him to waltz. Her blond American learned but stumbled. Then another soldier tried to cut in.

For some reason, Father told me later, this Granić went into a rage. A fight ensued. Apparently there was bad blood. We never knew whether Margit had deceived him, but she soon lost her soldier. Whatever they had was slowly poisoned. Soon after that a girl leaped from the north bridge into the Salzach River. Our camp gossips jumped to one conclusion: Margit Massong.

When Father asked Mother, she said, "I felt so bad for Nanschi. Fortunately we soon realized it wasn't Margit at all."

It turned out the victim was a pregnant girl from upstream Wolfskirchen, deserted by her American boyfriend. All the same, almost overnight Nanschi, her daughter Margit and her little brother Rudi all left for Salzburg. Rumor had it that soon after they signed on to emigrate to South America—Colombia to be exact. It needed people. During recess I looked up Colombia in Fräulein Seebach's *Methodical Atlas.* Within its dated borders, worlds south of North America, I found hellholes like Barranquilla. Somewhere on the steaming coast, where pasts didn't matter.

As my knowledge of America grew, I began to study the American garrison. One day after school, still digesting the news of Margit, I passed the fenced compound. A little girl in a hooded coat shrieked at me through the wire fence. Something about me must have enraged her—maybe my American coat.

"*Deutscher, ich dich schlagen tot!*"

Her broken German sounded vaguely Russian. I must have looked puzzled. I wasn't exactly German, being from the Balkans. I wasn't even Austrian, and I'd never fought American troops. She was prettier than my Austrian classmates, even Monika Waldegger, and maybe some colonel's daughter. But again she hissed in her German:

"German, I'll hit you dead!"

I studied her through the wire mesh, my face centimeters from hers. Her pretty eyes were porcelain blue. I'd become interested in America. I relished *Classics* comic books and dreamed of the Wild West, and I was discovering English words and even the boxer Jersey Joe. I was at the beginning of a lifelong study of America. Out of curiosity, I tried out some English I'd picked up from the soldiers.

She looked blank. I didn't know what the words meant, and apparently she didn't either. Coming from soldiers, they probably meant nothing good. Still curious, I said the words again.

"*Fuck you.*"

This time she blinked.

CHAPTER 14

THE THIRD MAN

During the day The Golden Jug was empty. As I glanced around the smoky walls, a clutch of trophy antlers testified to some hunter's fortune, probably that of Josef Gstaltmeier, the bygone innkeeper. A folksy hat hung from one point, and a sluggish fly buzzed overhead. Through the windows I glimpsed chestnut trees. I can't recall who got me word, but I'd been told to report to the widow, Frau Luise Gstaltmeier. I sat down at an oaken corner table from where I could see the door. The stuffed stag's head above me seemed to grunt in dismay. Somehow it fit with my waiting to be fed.

Now Luise Gstaltmeier entered with a plate of soup and a slice of bread. The dry bread wasn't even remotely fresh, a far cry from Frau Hollinger's. She asked my name as she plopped things before me.

"Konrad."

"*Lass dir's schmecken,*" she said in dialect. "Enjoy your meal."

She looked unenthusiastic, but I soldiered on. My job was to fill out and put meat on my bones. I broke the bread into the soup to soften it and also give the soup more body. It was basically a vegetable broth with isolated bobbing peas, carrot slices, and potato cubes. I wouldn't get fat at Luise's, but it was a change from the camp's black bean soup, and every little bit helped. I didn't have to like her sparse charity. I thought of my camp neighbor, Norbert, and his tin spoon and started ladling. The lantern-faced shit had all the luck. Luise turned back toward her kitchen, her bony frame choked by her apron. As her head with its tight gray bun disappeared inside the kitchen, a workman by the back door called to deliver cases of beer. That part fit, since the inn was named The Golden Jug.

I checked the stag's snout above me. It looked dusty, so it wouldn't drool. I ladled slowly as the fly droned. On the way uptown I'd seen Herr Gruber shuffle toward his own inn, Zum Hirschen. He'd looked too absorbed to notice me as I hurried toward my free lunch. Unfortunately I'd also seen Norbert from the next partition dodge into Frau Hollinger's bakery. My antennas bristled.

Someone had gotten Straubling's merchants to sponsor a summer feeding program for us refugee children. I suspected the Reverend Dachnagl, whose special charge was refugees. It was a pious thing to do but had unintended side effects.

During school all of us children, including the Austrians, had that polenta in the cafeteria. The boiled ground corn was filling, but the summer vacation was a wasteland. Now each refugee was assigned his own inn or shopkeeper to visit for a daily lunch. Norbert had drawn Frau Hollinger, and over my soup his good fortune haunted me. I dreamed of fried veal schnitzel. By now, I imagined, he'd emerge from her tidy bakery picking his square chops.

I cursed softly.

From now on he'd be feasting surrounded by Frau Hollinger's fragrant buns, while I ladled at Luise's. Although her place was called The Golden Jug, it was clear she would offer nothing fancy, ever. Only the weak soups and gruels she'd plop before me. And although some contained farina, they were served with yesterday's rye, despite the trophy antlers suggesting venison.

My dumb bad luck amazed me. Even though Frau Hollinger liked me, Dachnagl's lunch program had somehow matched her with Norbert. When I saw him emerge one day, my curiosity ran away with me. His news surpassed my worst imaginings. As I ladled he'd feasted on sausage and potato salad, sometimes even tender wienerschnitzel, followed by a vanilla scoop. I could have smacked him.

"Something wrong?" he said innocently.

I could barely conceal my outrage, but didn't want to let him gloat.

"You've got something in your eye," I lied. "And Milan?" I continued, as if greedy for more punishment.

The beetle-browed little Croat feasted on roast and purée at the butcher's, attested Norbert. In other words at Ponkratz's, Gustl's father. The same Gustl I'd once tripped. I gnashed my teeth. Of course, I couldn't be caught eating at Gustl's, not with our dirty little secret; even his country cousins Naz and Poldi wouldn't. But I wished for Norbert and little Milan to get lost in the vast spaces of Canada or Australia. No chestnut trees stood on those plains, like the magnificent one before Frau Hollinger's.

"What's the matter?" mocked Norbert, his green eyes guileless.

I felt my jaws clench. "Don't overdo and gorge yourself. You'll want to stay in shape for hockey. If you ever get to Canada."

"Why wouldn't I?" he said.

He didn't even bother to deny that it lay in his future, if his granny's plans held up. As he skipped off, he hummed the popular little tune that made the rounds just then. All the refugees in camp hummed it, even Vera Kratky, whistling out of that puffy mouth. Not to mention the locals. It cried out for zither music, although not at bony Luise's:

Mariandl,-andl,-andl
Du hast mein Herz am Bandl, Bandl,
Du hältst es fest und lässt
Es niemals wieder los.

Mariannie,-annie,-annie,
You tug my heart strings, heart strings,
You hold my heart so tight
You'll never, ever let it go.

I had better things to do than singing. They included seeing films whenever Father spared me change—preferably American films—as well as adventure tales, school, chess, and Ludwig's drawings. And first and foremost now the American boxer, Jersey Joe, whom I'd seen fight in a newsreel, and always, of course, finding interesting things to eat. Still, I ate whatever I could get my hands on, just as I'd read anything, especially the *Classics Illustrated*.

Mother and Father had their hands full making the eating possible. I liked eating in itself, but also to hasten my growth spurt. The camp's black bean soup was mere lining for our stomachs, only a notch above Luise's. You couldn't trust the camp supervisor, Gustav Finger, to have even horse meat sprinkled in, much less trust his cook, Toni Spitz. Despite this or because of it, every few months Mother and Father still went dancing. At Stubaier's, as I said, which Mother literally knew from the ground up. She scrubbed his pine dance floor and made up the upstairs rooms, except those evenings when she and Father waltzed.

That's when they, too, first heard the little ditty set to zither music, about some peasant hankering for a girl he missed.

I guessed that when they all danced to Mariandl they held her in their hearts. Mother and Father and Florian Riedl, with his girlfriend Vroni, and slimy Toni Spitz with his Ilon, but mostly townsfolk and peasants, along with Yankee soldiers and the Serb Royalists all competing for the local girls. One of them might have been the floozy, Margit, squeezed by her American. It was probably at Stubaier's that she'd first met Matt Granić. Anyway, over the next days and weeks everyone hummed Mariandl's little melody, so who was I to argue?

Only one thing just then competed, due to its zither music—a haunting film set in Vienna. I was desperate to see *The Third Man* because it was American; at least I thought it was, although most people seemed drawn more by its zither music and two popular Austrian actors in it, Anni Rosar and Paul Hörbiger. The film being American, their parts must have been minor. Unfortunately I already knew I wouldn't get to see it. The theater rated it for adults, no doubt with church approval. There was no way Father would give me change or let me go even if the usher might turn a blind eye and let me in. No ushers ever turned blind eyes. Father did promise to tell me about the film afterward.

Anyway, films made life exciting. And you never knew about the newsreels that came before them. Sometimes they were best of all, like the first time I saw Jersey Joe Walcott's hammering fists. I'd squeeze through the crowded theater lobby to the ticket booth for one of the cheap front-row seats that actually made films more dramatic by forcing you to crane your neck. Films mattered even more because everywhere you went you had to push.

Working all her odd jobs, for example, Mother was so busy she had me shop for milk and groceries. And at the farmers' co-op, you had to push toward the counter. When the clerk finally took an order, those who flailed and pushed hardest always got their bids in first. "Please, a liter of milk!" they shouted, or "Three eggs!" Ration cards for an item made the crush worse. Only Frau Hollinger's bakery was a small sanctuary; she respected everyone. I had strong legs, Mother would flatter me, proud of how I coped. I considered coping less, but something always pushed me forward to snatch a challenge.

In its small way, it was a momentous summer, despite the prods and pushing. When it ended, so did Luise's free lunch. But I got some satisfaction. After jostling at the milk counter I waited at Dr. Deutlinger's to see about a tooth. Mother cleaned there, so we got a special rate. Even as I waited, I could almost smell his sour breath as he leaned over me with his steel probe. Some tooth of his own needed pulling. I recalled Mother saying how he marveled at black American soldiers' strong white teeth, and his dismay when some wanted healthy front teeth capped with gold.

"Criminal," he would huff, even though after the war getting dentists' gold was probably his biggest problem. "And all for show. Worse, it's a sin."

Just when my time came, an adult marched in, demanding to be next. "I have some urgent business; it can't wait." It was Luise Gstaltmeier.

After her thin soups, now she used her status against me. Dr. Deutlinger, of course, took her; adults always came first. I prayed for her to have festering cavities.

When I said hello, she barely recognized me, but I could see one cheek was swollen. She went in ahead of me, and the groaning began. Her bony frame seemed to rattle in the dentist's chair like a dried-out chestnut pod. When she finally came back out, Luise looked pale and wet. Despite my own throbbing tooth, I dodged cheerfully around her. For sure, my tooth didn't ache from her soup. It turned out to be nothing. After the doctor yanked it, I felt foolish but easier. That evening I got Father to promise not only to tell me about *The Third Man*, but to let me see Douglas Fairbanks in *Sinbad the Sailor*.

CHAPTER 15

ALMOST FORGETFUL

When *The Third Man* finally came to Straubling, it had that pulsing zither music. The moviegoers were abuzz. I was sure Father would have his own tart perspective.

"Your hero did as expected," he told me afterward.

I must have looked puzzled since I hadn't seen the film.

"Ezzard Charles. In the newsreel before the film."

"He's not my hero," I said. "I wanted Joe Louis to stay champion. Nobody deserves to replace him. Is this Charles supposed to be the new champion?"

"Apparently," said Father. "Hard decision over a journeyman, that fellow Walcott. You seem to know him. It took all of fifteen rounds, though. Walcott didn't hand him the victory."

"He'll win it eventually. Jersey Joe's not a quitter."

"Ah, so you know his nickname? Too bad you couldn't see the feature," he added, "but I don't think you would have liked *The Third Man*. A little heavy, even for a rascal like you. Grim scenes of occupied Vienna. You would have liked one scene, though, atop the giant Ferris wheel. Maybe someday you'll see the film. And Vienna's worth a trip if the Russians ever leave."

Vienna didn't sound so different from Salzburg or even Straubling. The same leaky roofs, ration cards, the trade in smokes and nylons, probably more moldy beets and potatoes, and cripples everywhere, just like Franz and Ludwig.

"Who's the hero?" I asked.

"There's no real hero, only a black marketeer. An American at that. But a good fit for Vienna, a real *strizi.* Very smooth and evil. Your mother liked the zither music but not the film. The romance had gone sour. But the slick American gets what he deserves. A police chase through sewers with dogs and flashlights."

Although the character was an American, it didn't sound like a film I would have enjoyed. But the last part sounded real.

"What about Paul Hörbiger?" I asked about the Austrian actor in it.

"Just a glorified doorman, but the audience loved him. Anyway, some good news," added Father. "Tomorrow I'll bring you a copy of the *Salzburger Nachrichten.*"

"The daily!"

"You can read all about the fight. Think your reading skills are up to it?"

They were, and I told him. He rapped me playfully across the face. "Then you can tell me all about it, and I'll give you change for *Sinbad.*"

"You've already promised that!"

True to his word, shortly afterward he gave me the coins, and I looked forward to some serious swashbuckling. The next day, though, when he brought the paper, I first spread the *Salzburger Nachrichten* over the folding cot where I slept and kept my things. Father had traded Herr Gruber's old bunk bed for the army cot to give us more room. Mother heated up some black bean soup, adding sliced onion, and before Father let me read the paper he sent me out for fresh bread. Since the errand was to Frau Hollinger's, it was a chore I relished. I didn't even resent her feeding Norbert all that summer. It wasn't her fault, just Dachnagl's timing.

After we'd eaten, Father took the front page and gave me the rest. I studied the sports page but at first found nothing on Ezzard Charles. Finally I found a tiny paragraph on his decision over Jersey Joe, not enough for real flavor. It did seem to have been a tough decision, so probably Charles wasn't that worthy. No one was worthy to follow Louis, except for one brief moment, Schmeling.

"Did you ever see Max Schmeling fight Louis?" I asked Father.

Father looked up absently. "Schmeling and Louis? When Schmeling won, people were beside themselves. But didn't Louis fight mostly later?"

For once he was wrong, even though I think as a young man he'd followed boxing. My interest in boxing amused him.

"Look it up," he added, referring to Louis. "Find out when."

Sometimes Father could be frustrating. Or maybe again he was testing me.

"Who would know?" I asked.

"Check at school, of course. It won't be in her atlas, but your teacher will help you find it elsewhere. She'll appreciate your curiosity." Before returning to his front page, Father added, "Don't forget, curiosity's the starting point for everything—all human invention. Even boxing. It'll help you in America. And my definite impression," he said, grinning, "is that you're curious as a cat."

Mother beamed but tried to hide it. No sense spoiling me, I think she thought. Her face had the same guarded expression Fräulein Seebach wore when the boys in our class amused her with some mischief.

"It'll get him in trouble, and soon enough."

Father had bigger fish to fry, or rather, potatoes. At first he pinched every *schilling* and would only periodically bring home copies of the *Salzburger Nachrichten*, maybe as gifts from his foreman. But eventually he gave in and subscribed. He wanted to follow world events, but I think also got it for me. He wanted me to read, but not American comic books, and the scarce material made reading a prize and privilege. It didn't matter that the Americans, as someone told him, had actually started the paper in 1945 to give Austrians more balanced news. Across the top it said *Salzburger Nachrichten* in dark, squat Gothic letters.

Soon after, only months after the Chinese crossed Korea's thirty-eighth parallel, I would study our new paper with ferocity, especially sports and world conflicts. Free-loading Norbert soon asked to borrow it for the ski jumping results. And Stipe Baumann, who I didn't think knew much German, once asked us for individual pages before we'd even finished them. All that would end, I thought, if we ever moved into a separate little place away from the camp, as Mother wanted. In the meantime the paper's reports on Korea never failed to anger Father. He wouldn't let me forget that day the Chinese had crossed the thirty-eighth parallel.

"The Communist hordes advance," he'd growl. "They're replacing the Nazis. Is this what's meant by 'Allied victory?'"

And then it happened, something I don't think ever got in the paper. At least I never saw it. It happened the one day I didn't get to the American dump ground. It gave me a jolt, although my not being there was probably lucky for me. Despite having my tooth yanked, weeks later I still ached. When I again ended up at Dr. Deutlinger's, he found a curious permanent molar erupting crookedly through the gap left by the old. It was too large and far too early to be a wisdom tooth.

Deutlinger sounded impressed. "It's unique but strong. But not to worry. Just chew on it normally, that'll help rotate it into place."

He must have sensed my doubts.

"The swelling will go down, and the gums will heal around it."

Mother would be relieved. She'd feared inflamed tonsils. Not just for any damage they might cause, but because she worried about medical costs that Father's employer might not pay. For once no one, not even Luise Gstaltmeier, had barged in ahead of me. But just then, as I sat in the dentist's chair with my mouth gaping like a carp's, that's when it must have happened.

Unknown to me, little Jiři Kratky, Milan, Norbert, and the rest of the gang had run to the American dump ground at Berti Krummbacher's call. It was their last chance that year to prospect. Fall was again approaching, and soon a first snow would dust the foothills. That afternoon little Jiři lost his footing and slid down the sloping trash heap toward the Salzach River. It all seemed to happen in slow motion, as a hushed Berti told it later, yet too fast for the others to stop him. We all felt guilty and responsible—even I, who wasn't there.

Jiři barely cried out. At the water's edge, almost forgetful, the turbid river scooped him up. A week later workers found his water-logged body downstream, pinned in the iron grate meant to strain out bulk objects as the Salzach rushed north to Salzburg, through the stone chasm it had carved out over time.

Mother said she would never forget Vera Kratky running screaming along the riverbank, as if that would cause the Salzach to disgorge him. His wide-eyed playmate Hedwig Hutz stood by in her soiled dress, not yet fully understanding what had happened. Vera cried out like a tormented animal. "Jiři! My little Jiři, come back!"

I'd miss his black button eyes, always alert and watchful. That evening Father had an odd look. "What are you growing, a shark's tooth? It can't be a wisdom tooth."

Something bad was coming.

"That damned tooth just might have saved you."

"He wasn't there, Hans," said Mother, trying to soften his anger.

Father's eyes grew cold and hard. "Anni, that's not the point. From now on, Konrad, no more poking in the American dump."

CHAPTER 16

DREAMS AND AMBITIONS

It was a crisp October day. White-capped peaks surrounded us, and the season's first snow had dusted the foothills. The chestnut trees on the square stood in fiery color. When their spiky pods dropped to the cobblestones they burst open, spilling glistening chestnuts.

"Let's go see who's died," said Herbert Mautner.

That meant the cemetery, just a short hop after school. I must have looked like a squirt walking next to Herbert, the tallest in our class. Each of his steps equaled two of mine, so he never seemed in a hurry. I awaited my growth spurt with some skepticism. For now, as Father sometimes joked, I must have looked squat and hard-bitten, like the local peasants. Herbert's blond hair and clear eyes, in the meantime, masked a taste for the macabre. I liked his quirks. There were two kinds of people—those you could trust and those who lied—and I trusted Herbert.

He meant no disrespect toward the dead but knew one day he'd be a surgeon. "I heard old Greiff kicked over," he continued. "Let's go see him."

Entering by the wrought-iron gate, we saw fine snow powder the letters of the headstones and linger below the evergreens. The firs, hedges, and junipers rose dark green among the stones. The snow and white gravel on the paths made the scene pristine and stark. Among the trees a road led to the chapel straight down from the gate. The copper cross on its slate spire rose against the snowy Alps. It was picture-postcard scenery.

When prominent locals died, they'd lie in state before their funerals. During the week townsfolk dropped by the chapel to pay their respects. Finally Simon Dachnagl, our instructor in religion class, would hold the funeral service. Preceded by his altar boys and trailed by the mourners with the casket, he would begin his stately march toward the freshly opened grave. Swinging his brass censer, he dictated the pace. His two altar boys in white lace collars and red skirts looked pious and mute.

Sure enough, in the chapel we found old Rudolf Greiff, resting in his open casket looking waxen like his candles. I recalled him from the grain merchant's, his son, where Father worked two weekends repairing the cellar. It was off-the-books black market work, but we could use the money.

When I brought Father soup in his canteen, Papa Greiff's head popped out a window over his boxed geraniums. He liked to check on Father and the family's helper from the South Tyrol, a migrant named Luigi Ponti. He claimed Luigi was no worker, just Italian and not even Tyrolese. All the while the younger Greiff's wife would throw thick soup bones to the family's growling mastiffs. As if to even the score, Father and Luigi spiced their lunch with wine by threading a thin hose into a cellar cask and sucking hard. Papa Greiff would have been furious if he'd known.

Now his cheeks looked sunken, all the more for being toothless. Somehow his lack of teeth made me think of the two dogs, all snout and fangs, facing off over the soup bones. At Papa Greiff's feet burned a tray of candles on black, cast-iron spikes. A few empty candle spikes invited visitors to light more stubs. Herbert crossed himself to show respect, in case adults happened by.

"Just as I expected," Herbert said.

"What are you looking for?" I asked.

Herbert leaned close to inspect the gray film of stubble on the dead man's jowls. He checked the fingernails of Papa Greiff's folded hands.

"The nails still growing, for example," he said cryptically. When I looked surprised, he said even dead bodies still had small reserves of nail protein, already formed before death. "It's all part of aging, although the signs aren't scientific."

It was news to me. "You're trying to get used to medicine?"

"Won't cure old age," he said modestly. "But might be the thing for me."

Herbert seemed surer than that. He was a rarity, who already knew what he would do and was smart enough to do it. I thought about Father's wanting me to read and his amusement when I followed boxing. For sure he'd never let me box; it wasn't why you went to America. But what he didn't know about was art and Ludwig's lovingly sketched behinds. I looked around a little nervously, as if he listened in.

"Art might be mine," I said carefully, defending myself against Father's invisible presence. "I'm just not as sure as you. My father probably wouldn't like it." I didn't know how they studied art in America, so I guessed. "I'd probably have to study anatomy, just like you."

Herbert's eyes lit up. "Good idea! You draw the living; I'll dissect the dead."

I tried to sound wise. "Aren't you supposed to save the living?"

"Autopsies get you ready."

We left Papa Greiff and toured the headstones, each telling its own tale. Our book bags bounced on our backs as we circled granite markers. The white gravel crunched beneath our shoes as we approached a twisted juniper.

"There's Andreas Brunner. He died just last year," Herbert said with gusto, pointing at the stone below the juniper. "Mangled by his tiller working his fields. A cold morning. He was drinking to stay warm."

His imagination was as bloody as mine, although I leaned toward vigilantes tracking murderers and horse thieves, or that Scottish adventurer in *The Master* reclaiming his ancestral home. My favorite priest, Klaus Sekyra, had told me the plot. Herbert remained our class clinician. He showed the same detachment when little Jiři drowned, even when I mentioned Vera Kratky running along the Salzach River.

"Maria Mautner, 1874–1948. Seventy-four," I reckoned, studying the porcelain portrait on a headstone. Fräulein Seebach's arithmetic proved handy. "And Josef Mautner, solicitor: 1869–1915. What was he doing soldiering at forty-six?"

Herbert looked at me. "It was a hard fall from a horse. Nothing to do with the war. Aren't you wondering about Maria's name?"

"You must be related."

"She died just recently. She was my great-aunt and would have outlived him anyway. Even back then women did," he said, "if they didn't die in childbirth. It was Semmelweiss who fixed that."

I wanted to ask about Semmelweiss. "The Viennese doctor," he anticipated. "Insisted doctors wash their hands before entering the delivery room. Not just wash them, use soap." He spied another plot. "There's Matthias Hollinger! A ripe old age: 1853–1945."

His headstone said "master baker." "Frau Hollinger's father?" I asked him.

It felt odd and slightly ominous to see the name of someone I knew, especially that of kindly Frau Hollinger, always there for me, like her warm bread and pretzels. As luck would have it, just now I spied her in the distance, carrying a vase of flowers. She wore a perky hat, the same traditional style as the emperor's rumpled suit, gray trimmed with green, but it couldn't contain her gray hair entirely. She must have stopped to tend her father's grave. I checked the exact date on the tombstone. Today was his birthday.

I pulled Herbert aside, feeling guilty. "Let's go; we're intruding."

Out of nowhere, up burped my nagging memory of Norbert Pfeifer at her bakery, gorging on veal and vanilla ice cream.

"What's the matter?" Herbert said.

He must have seen my jaws clench.

Before she saw us, we had moved far from Frau Hollinger to find a white stone obelisk overarched by shadowy junipers. I'd seen it before, although not with Herbert. It resembled the one I'd seen last year with Berti Krummbacher. A white stone curb with black cast-iron chains confined the plot of soil. Near the top of the white obelisk glowed a blood-red hammer and sickle, from which a ladder of chiseled text descended down the slender stone. The dark characters looked Cyrillic; I knew their shapes from the Balkans. Below the Russian text followed a brutal translation:

In Memory of our Soviet comrades, murdered by the Fascists.

"Are you surprised?" said Herbert.

I wasn't. I already knew about the Soviet prisoners from our gossipy neighbor, Berti, and even from Father. The grim knowledge floated in the air like fog seeking to alight. I didn't want to let it. Having escaped Tito's prison camp with Mother, I thought I understood the Russians' predicament. But I didn't want to think too hard about them. I couldn't have done anything, and I didn't know who could have. Their former camp downstream from ours spilled over Alois Lechner's fertile bottomland, where the Nazis held the POWs before the Americans held their maneuvers there.

When I'd first come across the camp site by accident, I wasn't quite sure what I was seeing. It looked like a pasture sleeping, just waiting to be worked.

CHAPTER 17

THE RUSSIAN PRISONERS

Berti had shown me around the year before. He lacked Herbert's imagination but saw a chance to impress with his superior knowledge of the bygone prison camp. It was October, just as it was a year later at the cemetery, but dark with clouds. Mists rose from the Salzach River, shrouding Lechner's fields. The early snow flurries melted almost as soon as they flecked the mud and blades of grass. One of Lechner's farmhands had driven cows across the pasture, once the Russians' camp; you could tell by their frozen droppings. The ground was half-frozen, yet the mud still sucked at our hobnailed boots. Back in our camp the roof had begun to leak.

My classmate Herbert and the gossipy Berti couldn't have been more different. He was our refugee camp's downstream neighbor in the switchman's yellow house by the railroad tracks. We tolerated each other and he had that view straight across the river, giving us all a head start whenever the American army's dump truck pulled up.

In fact, for the last time that year, Berti and I had just finished prospecting in the American dump. Soon snow would cover its treasures and make its slope more treacherous. Father hadn't yet said "no," and little Jiři wasn't dead. Berti and I weren't ready to go home and decided to walk near Lechner's. As we headed toward his sheds and barn I saw the cropped fields in the mist. Farther down along the river, Lechner worked his fields. The former Russian camp lay closer, its northern stretch now the American maneuver grounds. Ruts and sod torn by the Americans gashed the foggy terrain. Wherever the ruts scoured the campsite, they exposed odd soggy strips.

Berti whispered for effect. "See those shreds of prisoners' uniforms?"

I didn't particularly want to touch them. Berti was trying to impress, as always. An oblong metal box lay on its side nearby, sticking out rusting legs. It had an ugly utility. I thought I knew what it had been. "A camp stove," I guessed.

Berti didn't react directly. "Lechner's a slowpoke," he said, superior. "I'm surprised he hasn't cleared out this junk. It must hamper his tilling. Right now he just grazes his herd."

"Why should he till?" I said, being practical. "If they're still maneuvering?"

"Smart-ass," said Berti.

I ignored him and said brutally, "Where did they bury them?"

Berti pointed toward the nearby railroad tracks. A clump of elders stood by the embankment over a mound of soil. I saw the earth faintly, shrouded by mist.

"Let's go see," I said.

"I've been there. You go," Berti said. "I'll check the maneuver ground."

He tramped forward in his hobnailed boots. As their soles collected mud, he flung out his legs, like barnyard fowl flicking their feet. Mine clotted too as I worked my way toward the burial mound. The plot's lumpy soil looked raw and frozen but was invaded by sparse tufts of grass. The thin obelisk in its center was a monument just like the one I'd seen later with Herbert, again with its blood-red star. Its black text had the same style and same message about the Soviet prisoners. I went back to it the following spring, when the elders bloomed and a train rushed by.

Now Berti stopped tramping and shouted through the mist. "Come on. There's lots to see," he cried, again eager to impress.

Beyond him I spied willows down by the river, faint fingers that rose through the fog. Berti seemed to want to play the tour guide to whatever American things he found; Herbert would have scoffed. We caught up to each other on the gashed terrain as the mud tugged at our steps. Not to be trumped by Berti, I found a muddy water flask resembling Father's old tin canteen. But his was broad and deeper and made for food, not drink.

"That's from the Americans. But I'll take it," I said.

"Saw it first," Berti countered. "A little dented, but good to hold my cartridges."

I didn't believe him. "Live ones? The hell you say."

"Told you there's lots to find here," he triumphed. "I probably shouldn't have shown you."

I saw his regrets, but the desire to show off overcame them. "Look, there's casings right here," he said, pointing to brass glinting in the mud.

"Just spent shells," I scoffed. "So what?"

"Except once I found those live ones," Berti bragged. "I keep those hid. My old man would kill me if he knew."

I recalled hearing about two boys killed playing with a rusting shell, this one German. They'd found it in a creek bed and decided to blow it up. In fact it was near Wolfskirchen, the same town whose pregnant girl had jumped off the northern bridge. Berti should have known not to be this dumb. I understood his fascination but I had far too much reading I wanted to do. I could get enough killing by tracking horse thieves in the wilds of Arkansas. I wouldn't take dumb risks.

Having survived the war, I doubted Father would have been impressed by Berti, either. "Idiot," I said.

Still proud of his cartridges, Berti scowled. "Watch your mouth."

"Your father would be right to kill you for a fool. If I don't hear the bang first."

He squinted at me, mouthing the words for Balkan trash. I looked right through him, daring him to say it out loud. But I wanted something that day too, a souvenir of my own. I dug two shiny spent casings from the mud and dropped them in my pocket, where I already carried an American mess spoon from the dump ground. The metal objects jingled together and seemed to bring me luck. Right away I found a trail of empty Coca-Cola bottles and then two full ones, mud-caked but dark red.

I pounced; now I was king. "Finders, keepers."

"You owe me for showing you around," said Berti.

I scraped the mud off the bottles. Before we could argue we heard a cart squeak and horses snort. Their breath steamed in the cool damp air. The sounds came from Lechner's barn along the river bend. Then we smelled a load of pungent steer manure. A voice called through the mist.

"What are you two rascals up to?"

It was a familiar voice—Alois Lechner's. He'd caught us before, stealing apples from his trees.

"What the devil do you want?" he shouted.

Now his high cheekbones and cropped mustache emerged from the ghostly mist. They set off his sharp nose, which didn't fit the rest of his face. Perched on his cart he looked like a bird of prey. A peasant like most locals, he was used to plowing and carting dung, but I wondered why he carted manure this late in October. Maybe it was meant to steep and ferment, to prepare the soil for spring plowing. Working his fields down along the river, maybe he feared we'd steal his last shriveled apples.

Now Lechner spotted me for who he thought I was.

"*Und du, zugroasta!*" he spat. It was the usual insulting word for foreigners—whoever didn't belong. The same one used by Naz and Poldi. "You get the hell going!"

The slimy word pursued me everywhere, even on this foggy maneuver ground. I felt a rush of spite, and I had two full Coca-Cola bottles. Thick and squat, they were just right to sling and throw. I thought about it for a second, feeling the bottles burn in my hands. But throwing them would have caused me serious mischief. Father would have been even angrier than if I'd blasted live shells. Besides, they deserved drinking. I'd get back at Lechner another way.

I tossed one bottle to Berti, and we scampered.

Back in the cemetery one year later, Herbert and I still studied the Russian monument under the junipers. "No dates," he said dryly. "It's just a marker. Even so, below these trees it's easy to miss. The plot's not big enough to hold all the bones."

I recalled the prisoners' mound by the railroad tracks and tried to sound detached. "They're buried near Lechner's."

"You're right. Nobody talks about it."

As we left the cemetery Herbert added, "Heard of Jabuka, one of the guards?"

I'd heard nothing even from Berti. Herbert still had all the good stuff. I'd hear more about Otto Jabuka and his shovel and not just from Herbert. Lechner must also have known him, if reluctantly. In the meantime Herbert told a good yarn as always—this one about Jabuka, a yarn grimly beautiful, like the one about the buried soldiers.

CHAPTER 18

THE THIRTY-EIGHTH PARALLEL

In the middle of winter Sepp Blassmann grabbed Toni Spitz by his tie and began pulling it tight. Sepp and Father had been comrades since the previous winter when they shoveled snow off railroad tracks. The day was eventful, not just for the spectacle, but for Korea and remote lines on maps.

For me, as for Father, lines on maps were living things, and not only because I liked chess and drawing. Father didn't talk much about Korea's thirty-eighth parallel, but when he did, he made everything seem haunted and connected—the American garrison, the jaunty cartoon at school about recovery, our flight from the Balkans, and the Royalists and refugees dreaming of Canada or Australia. He made me recall Fräulein Seebach's *Methodical Atlas* of 1903, showing the bygone Austria-Hungary's borders that once contained our town. Once such lines were broken, Father said, they released refugees. Any changes in maps caused ripples, like last summer's news about Korea:

Chinese Cross Thirty-Eighth Parallel

Scowling at the headline of the *Salzburger Nachrichten*, Father had said, "They took it upon themselves to defend freedom. Now they need to prove it." He seemed to question America's resolve. "This is war," he added ominously, "not a cheap action."

A grainy newsreel helped me imagine the crossing, and at school I found Korea's thirty-eighth parallel in Inge Seebach's old atlas. That fall and winter, whenever the paper reported on Korea, I would visualize the

Red Chinese swarm south in their padded uniforms over the thin parallel, although they looked gray, not red. The new war in Korea was worlds away from Straubling, and it lasted longer than that one summer, long enough for cold and winter and for the Chinese hordes to need their padding. But as it turned out, despite Father's misgivings he had a surprise. The remote parallel proved happier for us than the new Balkan borders drawn up after World War I.

But first Norbert, Milan, and the rest of us watched open-mouthed when Sepp Blassmann twisted Spitz's black tie. We'd heard juicy rumors about Toni Spitz and Sepp's wife. It was cold outside, but we felt warm. As Sepp choked our camp cook, Spitz's face turned blue above his white kitchen apron. Meanwhile the chunky Blassmann, as he choked Spitz, spoke with him almost tenderly about his sins and transgressions. Putting all his weight behind him, he just about lifted Spitz off the barracks floor. From the audience Ludwig winked at me—lascivious—and urged Sepp on with his crutch.

Spitz's wife Ilon had disappeared, but Sepp's wife Mari cried out, her hair across her face. "Sepp, no! For God's sake, someone stop them!"

It was Father who stepped in to separate the combatants. He did so gently, as Sepp's friend and comrade and as one of the few able-bodied men in our camp. The others were too old, and Franz and Ludwig were crippled. Sepp was powerful like Father, his body like a tree trunk; Spitz by acclaim was a parasite. The rest of us were children or widowed women.

"Easy," Father coaxed Sepp. "Don't dirty yourself with him."

Sepp Blassmann looked up and then tugged harder. Again Spitz's snappy black tie tightened. By now I think Sepp relished the attention. He would tighten his grip, release it, and again wrench Spitz's tie, impressing his audience even more than by strangling Spitz.

"The shame of it will outlive him," farther said slyly. "It'll be a fitting punishment."

Sepp grunted as if seeing the justice in his words.

Finally Father's intervention allowed him to release Toni Spitz with honor. Our cook's round eyes stopped popping out, and he sputtered regaining his breath. He looked around as if seeking his patron, Gustav Finger. But our camp supervisor was nowhere to be seen, as though he feared his presence would release more turmoil. It all happened so quickly that Father hadn't focused on Sepp's audience.

Just when I felt most proud of him and of being a Kemper, Father ordered, "Get the children out!" He glared at me in particular. "You too, Konrad. Out!"

"And all because of that bitch," he told Mother afterward. That seemed to confirm the camp rumors. Apparently he meant Sepp's wife, Mari.

"There's enough fault to go around," Mother objected.

"It's bad enough that Spitz and Finger are stealing our rations," Father added, "all while pretending to do their duty. When's the last time we saw meat? And then the children have to witness such spectacles."

Apparently Spitz's descent had begun early, I learned from Father later. Back in Yugoslavia, he'd curried favor with the invading Nazis. Wherever opportunity knocked, Spitz wound up near those on top. It was the kind of collaboration that, when the war ended, cost other ethnic Germans throughout Eastern Europe. Now, as our camp cook, he was said to share our horse meat rations with Gustav Finger, a Sudeten German who'd been appointed our camp supervisor. Some inmates claimed Spitz even mopped Finger's brow as the beefy Gustav gorged.

"Mari and Spitz had a thing, didn't they?" Mother said in disgust. "She helped out in the kitchen, exposed to his oily charms."

"I'm sure it wasn't just his doing," Father said. He seemed to hold something against Sepp's wife, or was he merely taking Sepp's side? "Mari promised to be true. She should have sworn off the likes of Spitz before she married Sepp."

Now he spied me in the doorway.

"And you, mud rat," he said, using Herr Gruber's phrase, "you just had to take it all in? Next time let's see some dignity. Even in this lousy camp, act like a Kemper!"

He seemed to think I lusted for the seamier side of camp life, which could taint me before we ever got to America. Family pride spurred him on too.

"I couldn't help it," I protested. "Sepp pounced before we knew it."

I hoped little Milan wasn't listening. I must have whined just like him and recalled Father's words about him. How, no matter what, the little shit remained his father's joy.

"Sepp's a regular Jersey Joe," I added, recalling my newsreel hero.

"That one's always got his eyes peeled," Mother reacted with perverse pride. "Just like his grandpa when he was young: a rascal through and through."

Suddenly she wiped away a tear. She thought of Grandfather, whom we'd had to leave behind in Tito's prison camp. Grandfather Wendt was dead now, but in his prime I was sure he could have stopped both Spitz and Blassmann. Yet he had taken time for me and the alphabet. Mother looked proud yet tired standing over the black metal box of a stove Father had bolted together from wartime scrap. It was a contraption that even the other women now clamored to use.

Before I could bask in her approval, Mother added, "I'm warming up leftover soup. Go get bread."

Father gave me some schilling he kept in reserve. Refugees still got no unemployment money, so it was good he'd found work at construction sites. Only out-of-work locals got state assistance—the construction workers and loggers, as Father always reminded us. Once, on leaving the claims office in a rage, he had wrenched its door handle beyond repair.

Before I could get out the door he said, "Keep your nose clean."

CHAPTER 19

JERSEY JOE

I leaped through the snow like a colt, my nostrils flaring. My breath escaped as puffs of fog. From the southern bridge across the Salzach it was only minutes to Frau Hollinger's. My mouth began to water as I passed the emperor's inn, Zum Hirschen. Austria's crisp buns were the best, encrusted with kernels of salt. Frau Hollinger's fragrant loaves were even better. I sniffed the air. Just across the river glowed her shop lights; her door chimed when I entered. She wrapped a warm loaf in newsprint.

"Eat hearty, young man. And say hello to your mother."

She was always friendly, even to refugees. I still didn't feel right when I recalled the cemetery where Herbert and I saw her visit her father's grave. But as soon as I walked back out in the cold, the fresh warm loaf made my knees go weak. I checked the newsprint wrapper, to be sure it wasn't a page I hadn't yet read. As I did I sniffed fragrant crust. So far my nose was clean. But halfway through the short walk back to Mother's hot soup I couldn't help myself. I began to chew one crusty end. Oddly enough Father never scolded me for this, and Mother would just shake her head. But leaning at the barracks entrance, the crippled Franz chose to shame me.

"Couldn't wait, could you? Not once take your folks their hard-earned bread?"

That stung. Franz looked bitter but superior.

Suddenly it was irritating not to know his last name. I wanted to know with whom I dealt. And where was Ludwig, who in a way stood up for me? The war had crippled him too, but only Franz looked pinched. Ludwig had a malign gusto. Did it come from being able to both draw and play chess? Was that why Franz nagged me now, instead of bundling up in their cramped partition? Unlike the two invalids, the Serbian Royalists across the river who'd once danced in our barracks had escaped Tito with their limbs intact. Was it some lost scent that set Franz off, a whiff of skirts and dancers?

As he bickered, I forgot their chess and drawings. Inside the barracks I heard rustling as some of the women looked up to hear us argue. "What'll your father say," Franz sneered again, "when he chews his hard-won bread?"

I studied him across the broken crust. "What's it to you?"

Behind him women craned their necks; Vera Kratky raised her bullet head. In the beehive of the barracks all petty strife was honey.

Franz turned toward his audience, his face like a rat's. "Listen to his lip."

"Talk to my father," I hissed, "if you think it's your business."

That shut him up. But now I'd have to stay away from him and Ludwig for at least the next week. No chats below those penciled cheeks. No watching them play chess. My fond wish to take on Franz and jam his king down his thin throat would have to wait. He had evaded the challenge anyhow, ever since Ludwig had crushed me. Had something in my defeat made him wonder—some promise I didn't see? And where was Ludwig while Franz poked in my business? I could smell Mother's black bean soup and hurried past him and the women.

Mother shook her head when she saw my scarred loaf. But the soup was hot and ready. What's more, she'd sliced some onion in it for flavor. On the stove next to the pot I saw my spoon marked USN, which she used for measuring. My nostrils flared; my hand reached for the bread.

She rapped my fingers briskly. "First go find your father."

Father and Sepp talked down by the river, upstream from the latrine. Their breath fogged the air. Sepp looked lost, as if his world had collapsed.

I was hungry, but even then I could tell Sepp Blassmann was a simple man. He didn't seem to like his wife, much less Spitz, but like Father and Fräulein Seebach he was someone you could trust. Back in our hometown, by good fortune, he had inherited a plot of sandy soil just right for vegetable farming and followed in his family's footsteps. The thick hands choking Spitz had once planted spring potatoes.

Father did all the talking, his words consoling. "It was Spitz's fault; you know that. Whenever a war ends the scum rises to the top."

I barely heard him over the rushing Salzach, and he stopped as I approached. Putting an arm around Sepp's shoulders, he told me he'd soon come in.

Over my crisp loaf and the bean soup, the work of Spitz and Mari's hands, we finally ate. "Ah, something smells so fine," said a voice in the next partition, obviously meant to be heard. It was Norbert Pfeifer's granny, but Father ignored her.

"I have an uneasy feeling," he told Mother.

She gave Father one of those looks to remind him I was present, and the walls had ears. He changed the subject, but his voice held smoldering anger.

"Not to look too far ahead, but we can expect more snow to fall. Last winter we got lucky even though we had to shovel. This time the snow's not all. Expect the river to rise once the snows melt."

"Somehow we'll get through it, Hans," said Mother.

I suspected her of liking Austria. Father's stored-up anger grew, as if building due to Sepp. "This camp's right on a flood plain. It's just like the Austrians. To them we're second class twice over. First we're Germans from the Balkans, and now lousy refugees."

Mother didn't take his bait. "Spitz's wife is hiding from everyone."

"Poor Ilon. I'd be red-faced too. Sepp will be all right, though," Father added softly, as if Blassmann's misery were unrelated.

As our tin spoons tapped against our plates, I could almost hear Granny Pfeifer breathe against our thin partition. I thought I heard rustling.

"This stinking camp," Father continued. "Is it any wonder people emigrate, even to South America? Even Spitz with his pretensions. A lot of good that black tie did him in the kitchen or outside it."

Suddenly he turned toward me, and his voice dropped. He said the last thing I'd expected, but then he liked surprises. His news was momentous, like lightning in a dark storm. "But I have something for you, mud rat. Not that you deserve it. You've heard the Boban clan's off to Australia? And Wilma Hutz and brood will sail for Brazil?"

My ears perked up.

"Promise you'll keep this quiet, and I'll tell you to start dreaming."

I promised.

My hero, Jersey Joe Walcott, was our code word in case Granny Pfeifer's ear was stuck to our partition wall. "Prepare to meet your Jersey Joe," Father said dryly. "It's just a matter of time."

I gasped. Mother began to cry, I think because she knew.

"Remember the thirty-eighth parallel?" Father asked me. "Do you see a link?"

It seemed an odd thing to ask just then. "What does it mean for us?"

"Your mother's overjoyed," he said.

She didn't seem to be. Father's voice dropped to a whisper.

"I'm hearing rumors, which I'll check out in Salzburg. Eventually, you can be sure, the Americans will accept visa applications from former German soldiers. There's a new enemy farther east."

Mother ladled out the rest of the bean soup, favoring me over Father. Her hand shook the ladle. With my USN spoon, she sprinkled in diced onion. All at once I saw it, a new world like a chessboard with fields of black and white. The Chinese hordes had a purpose; old struggles were receding. Soon a new conflict would nudge us toward America. The Chinese would eclipse World War II in Europe and open the new world for old enemies.

That night I couldn't sleep, and neither did Father and Mother. They tossed in their bed opposite the stove along the other wall of our cubicle. My cot stood where Herr Gruber's bunk once stood. The emperor was gone now but probably wouldn't have slept much either. The cold air outside our window panes had frosted them with lacy flowers, and I heard ice floes clank on the Salzach River, the sound clean as chunks of glass under the starry sky. I liked winter.

Then I heard a muffled thumping down the hallway and a stool knocked over. People ran across the wooden floor. "I'd better see what's up," Father whispered and went out. "No need to call a gendarme," I heard him say down the hallway, near yet far away. "I'll talk to him."

When he came back he spoke to Mother, this time making no effort to spare me. He seemed tired. Last winter had been Mother's turn, when she got the news of Grandfather's death. Father seemed to be testing my ability to keep a secret. But I knew this wouldn't stay a secret.

"That poor dumb swine," he said. "They were just getting ready to join Sepp's brother in Australia. They'd better go while they can. Sepp just tried to hurt his wife."

CHAPTER 20

DISTANCE VISION

Despite his melancholy about Sepp Blassmann and his doubts about Korea, Father soon recovered his good spirits. Something was in the air—a cold clean smell that seemed to come with the snow. He always liked to say you should never get too comfortable. Now he seemed focused, even resolute about America, even if I couldn't always tell if he was serious or just testing me.

One evening as the snow fell, he said casually, "Speaking of your hero, Jersey Joe, did you know that in America they have radios that let you see?"

Mother was scrubbing the floor of Stubaier's dance hall uptown for some big event, so I was his captive. Father sometimes joked with her too. "The kid's a survivor, always thinking and scheming." So I was ready for surprises, and right off I saw an opportunity.

Father brought me back down to earth.

"In fact, if we had such a radio, you could probably see your Jersey Joe knock out this Ezzard Charles, or whoever else." But we didn't have such a radio, or any radio. "They're going to fight again, aren't they?" he added.

That July 18, 1951, was years away for all I knew. But if Joe won, as I expected, I'd be feverish in a different world: Jersey Joe's.

"Of course Joe's a serious challenger," I managed, "and he'll knock out Charles."

But I'd stopped ladling my soup. The idea of radios for distance vision was too astonishing, even more than Fräulein Seebach's paper handkerchiefs. I didn't even think to be surprised that Father knew about Ezzard Charles, the rival I wanted Jersey Joe to humble. With Norbert

Pfeifer one partition over, it was hard to escape his ski jumper, Bradl, but how could there be radios for seeing Jersey Joe box?

"How can that be?" I repeated.

Father winked. "Americans are far-sighted. They can even see events here in Europe, to the extent the Soviets will let them. Maybe even this lousy camp, to the extent they're actually interested." I thought I heard a trace of bitterness about America. "They may even see behind North Korean lines or into the future to prevent more invasions. To the extent God will let them."

He used the words *to the extent* like finishing nails. Each tapped into the coffin of my ignorance. I must have looked baffled. But now he playfully tugged my shoulder. I asked him how he knew about Charles.

Father laughed. "Newspapers. I make it my business to know." Our going to America wasn't really settled, but he acted as if everything was. "Besides, we'll soon be meeting Jersey Joe."

Joe remained our code for our arrangements for America. The walls and Granny Pfeifer had ears. I hoped Father considered going to New Jersey since he'd persuaded Mother. The Garden State, as it was called. All American states had their nicknames. It wasn't the wilds of Arkansas I'd read about, but it was Jersey Joe's New Jersey. But first I wanted to get at Norbert and saw an opportunity.

"Could these radios show Sepp Bradl jump all the way to Canada?" I asked him.

The new radios reminded me of Norbert's endless yammering about his hero, Sepp Bradl, the world-class ski jumper and his personal high flier. I hoped in Moose Jaw or wherever in Canada he finally ended up with his uncle, his sister Kati, and his snoopy granny, he'd find a worthy hero. Maybe a hockey player. Lantern-jawed Norbert belonged in Moose Jaw. He seemed taken by cold and snow; it was about all we had in common.

Father pretended not to understand. "I don't think even Sepp Bradl can jump all the way to Canada, but, yes, they could send pictures of him jumping to Canada. Or even New Jersey. Although I doubt Canadians would be that interested."

That would take care of Norbert.

"It's an amazing thing," I said. There remained the *Salzburger Nachrichten*. "I don't recall the paper ever mentioning distance vision, do you?"

"Full of questions, aren't you? What's up your sleeve?"

Father seemed to have a power of vision. He not only knew about distance vision, but he could see right through me. I dodged the question.

"I'm glad we have our own subscription now," I said.

"A big word, *subscription*. Excellent, Konrad."

"But it hardly ever mentions Jersey Joe. Gustl Ponkratz has a radio," I said hopefully.

Right away I regretted focusing his attention elsewhere. I thought Father might have heard the tired old news about my tripping Gustl. Fortunately he didn't bite.

"Oh, does he? Reading's much better," he said, "fires the imagination. Your teacher's taught you well. She's a fine woman, with a heart for refugees."

I shifted back to distance vision. "I'd rather see boxers fighting."

"Keep up the reading."

"Norbert can't read worth beans," I capitulated. "He only dreams about Bradl."

But the word *beans* reminded me. Beans were everywhere, especially in our soup. Father put a finger to his lips and motioned toward our neighbors' wall.

"A great sportsman," he proclaimed so the Pfeifer clan could hear, "and a hero of our time. Even back in the Reich they loved Sepp Bradl. In 1936 especially, when that American won at the Olympics. Only Jersey Joe's his equal."

I was inclined to agree. But before I could gloat about humbling Norbert with my news about distance vision, Father threw a bombshell. "Not only is Jersey Joe a model of courage, he's a son of immigrants."

Suddenly I wasn't sure about Joe. I'd wanted him to be pure American.

"But don't let that bother you," Father sympathized. "It means he came up the hard way. It's an American tradition we're sure to honor. What I want most for you, *strizi*, is to do well in school, do you hear? No need to box to climb the ladder. Be alert; you'll just about inhale the English.

One day soon you'll not only watch Jersey Joe on the new radios, but understand every word."

I wasn't so sure and returned to Joe's origins. "Where was he from?"

"The West Indies. I should say, his father."

"Where's that, in Africa?"

Father feigned ignorance. "You tell me. Look it up in your teacher's atlas."

But if he knew about Jersey Joe's being a son of immigrants, he probably knew about the Indies. The article would have said where. Again he was testing me. After my homework, before Mother got back, he lobbed another shell.

"And by the way, his real name isn't Jersey Joe, or even Joseph Walcott."

By now my brain was spinning. "What, then?"

That evening Father seemed to give out nothing for free. "Find out, so you can test me! But doesn't Jersey Joe sound hard and strong? Walcott sounds just as tough. All together, the name Jersey Joe Walcott packs a punch. For an American boxer, it's a knockout of a name."

I had to agree. But my plans for Norbert were crumbling. "Sepp Bradl uses his own name. Even though he's Austrian, he's as good as they get."

"That's Europe for you," Father said. "But isn't he also known as *Bubi*?"

I was relieved. "The kid?"

"Exactly. American boxers use that nickname, too. Many call themselves 'kid.'" He savored the English word. "Now go to sleep. Get primed for your growth spurt."

What growth spurt? Those weren't the words to make me sleep. I tossed, skinny and uneasy, full of plans for Norbert, just as eventually I saw myself on board a ship full of plans for America. The next morning I listened for Norbert in the next partition. I heard him fidget as Granny Pfeifer stirred up a mash of polenta, the same mash they fed us at school lunches to bulk up our diet. It wasn't only us refugees that needed nutrition. I didn't know where granny had gotten her ground corn, but the hot water came from the camp kitchen, and I smelled her mash cooking. Soon they would be feasting. Even so Norbert found the time to tease his older sister, Kati, hinting she had a boyfriend.

Her tongue was quicker. "No one would look at you."

She must have gotten her wits from her granny, who seemed too proud to scold her. Now I heard the old woman plop plates on their rickety table, like Luise Gstaltmeier during my summer feeding. Norbert dared to ask for a spoon.

"I'll spoon you in a minute," snapped his granny. "Make yourself useful, and lay out spoons for everyone!"

Soon they seriously clicked and ladled, not exchanging a word. No one mentioned distance vision—television—or even Jersey Joe or Sepp Bradl. Norbert must have missed Father's words the night before; he'd probably foraged for something interesting. I lay in wait for him outside the barracks. Before he could shuffle toward school, I locked eyes with his, like green buttons in his freckled face.

"Did you know that in America they have radios that let you see?"

"What are you talking about?"

"Distance vision. It lets you see events from afar."

"Can't be," flailed Norbert. "I've seen Sepp Bradl in a newsreel, but he wouldn't stoop to such a thing. He already has distance vision. Every time he jumps and soars he sees the ski slope and the crowd below him."

"But not all his fans can see him. He'd want all his admirers to see."

"It's another of your schemes. Such radios don't exist."

"All Americans have 'television.'"

Norbert's round green eyes became goggles. We were just passing the camp latrine. "You're shitting me."

"Nobody here can afford it, that's all. Another thing, Americans wouldn't show Sepp Bradl jumping. They'd show Jersey Joe stopping Ezzard Charles. Ski jumping doesn't interest New Jersey or even Canada."

"That can't be. When Sepp first broke one hundred meters, the whole world was in awe. Even today he's a legend."

"Bradl, Schmadl," I said. "They don't even use meters."

The Salzach ran beside us, its ice chunks smoking as they met warmer air above it.

"What, then?" huffed Norbert.

"I imagine you'll find out in Canada," I said as we neared school. "Isn't that where you're going? But you can be sure of one thing. In America they'll ski jump before they ever do up in Canada. If they're ever interested.

America's where things happen first. But if you get lucky, maybe you'll get to watch ice hockey. And your granny may fetch you a spoon."

Norbert flushed. "Bradl's the best, even if he is from Austria."

"We're not locals like him," I taunted. "Just lousy refugees."

Suddenly he cracked his bony left across my face and ran. Enraged, I took off after him. He was beating me at Jersey Joe's game. Norbert huffed as always, but the school building was close enough to give him refuge. Before I caught him he dodged inside.

In the evening Father had another surprise.

It was a letter from Stefan Marschall from our hometown, the one who'd stayed in nearby Wels during our time in Salzburg, now happily settled in Detroit. Or so he said. In Wels he had worked in that American mess hall and somehow, Father said, had parlayed this good fortune into what he called the "Motor City." Stefan's letter contained a snapshot and two clippings from an American magazine. In the photo he and his wife Mirjam—he now worked in an auto assembly plant—posed by their new car he proudly called a Chevrolet. They gazed into the distance like conquering heroes. They probably even had their own radio for distance vision.

Father looked bemused. "They've arrived."

I didn't want to look at them. More important to me were the magazine clippings. The first showed an earnest American family huddled before a box that stood upright and waist-high, like a large radio, with a small lit screen embedded in it. Distance vision! Stefan's second article contained a photo of Jersey Joe being humbled by Ezzard Charles. I burned with outrage but greedily accepted the clippings. They were my trumps over Norbert. No need to stoop to fists, I'd crush his spirit.

"All yours," said Father. "I told Stefan about your hero. The clippings have the facts I mentioned. I would have changed my name too, if I'd been Arnold Cream. You may think differently. But if you want more detail, you'll have to dig it out yourself and learn some English. But try to spare your mother!"

He laughed and turned toward her.

Mother had been darning socks through our discussion. Like the Marschalls she seemed pensive, as if dreaming of America. I could almost smell the fresh snow outside, a silent blanket that somehow helped keep us warm.

CHAPTER 21

GAMBITS

It was a slow avalanche just beginning. Soon I had more important business than Norbert or his Sepp Bradl.

But at first something felt wrong. Franz and Ludwig were giving me the shot I'd wanted. By now I finally knew their names from Mother: Franz Weiss and Ludwig Janko. Mother wasn't happy when I asked about them.

"What are you doing with that scum?"

I should have asked Father. "Just curious," I said and shrugged, secretly glad to have their names.

Somehow I thought it would help me make my moves to know with whom I dealt. As during my earlier chess match with Ludwig, snow again fell outside. It fell in sheets of silent white. I couldn't see the Salzach and the foothills, but the snow was prettier. When the time came for the match, an old stain on the invalids' floor planks showed where the roof dripped once the snow melted. I shut their warped partition door.

"This is just among the three of us," said right-legged Ludwig, his crutches against one wall.

"Fine with me," I said.

"No sense announcing it to your friend, Norbert, or the rest. It's the sport of kings. We have to do it justice." A little ominous, Ludwig's face was close to mine. "I'll referee."

Norbert wasn't my friend exactly, but I kept my mouth shut.

Franz glowered at me from his cot, the faded Wehrmacht coat slung over him. His crutches leaned behind him. One had a cracked leg around which he'd wound a coil of wire. I wondered where he'd found the rusty wire. Far away I could hear Norbert whine down the corridor, about some chores he didn't want. He thought his sister Kati should be the one to scrub the dishes. Luckily the snow muffled him and my gut's floating butterflies. As always I loved the silent snow—how it changed everything. It was my ally.

Franz and I arranged the pieces on the board with Ludwig perched inscrutably. Unlike earlier, Franz wouldn't concede me white. We drew lots, and I got black. He advanced his white king pawn. Right off, as I'd expected, I felt pulled into his web. In earlier games with Ludwig, I'd seen Franz was a defender, methodical even when he opened white. Now I felt his tightening coils. He didn't slash like Ludwig, and he lacked imagination. But for every move of mine he had an answer, a confining move that sucked me deeper. Eroding my space for maneuver, he squeezed me like a spider. My men were cramped and suffocating.

Then I got lucky.

It was the kind of mistake you make when you underestimate an opponent, especially one you see as a novice and a nuisance. It was my main strength. As soon as Franz had moved, Ludwig clucked. When I looked at him I thought he guessed the move I'd make. I think he saw me as an heir—a raw beginner but a pirate. Franz had made his error but didn't seem to know it until the cluck. Ludwig looked away, all innocence, to gaze at their familiar penciled drawings of plump female behinds. They circled the fading brown-papered walls like a rosary.

In trying to stifle me, Franz had castled and then advanced his eighth king-side pawn one notch. My heart plopped to my shoes. I slammed his pawn with my bishop along the white diagonal. Now he could take my bishop with the pawn that was meant to shield his king. But that would rip his king side open. Or he could choose not to capture but still leave his king side weakened.

Either choice was bad, and Franz didn't seem to know it. He took my bait right off, the sacrifice of my bishop. That shredded his king side and left my nearby queen and knight poised for the kill. Franz's own queen was stuck too far away behind his massive defenses. So were most of his pieces, choking of their own weight.

Again Ludwig clucked. Within minutes it was over. I ripped Franz's heart out just as Ludwig had ripped out mine. But I knew I'd gotten lucky. If Franz ever gave me a next time, I wouldn't get an inch. He wouldn't play me move by move but by overall position. No more taking me for granted. He said as much, though he looked baffled.

"I didn't think you had it in you."

"The kid's good for surprises," Ludwig approved.

"They'll carry him just so far. Steady's better in the long run."

Actually I agreed with that.

"Psychology's everything," Ludwig added. "He beat you fair and square."

"It's just a game."

"In this camp, games are everything. Right, kid?" concluded Ludwig.

Finally Franz extended his hand, an odd and calloused hand. I didn't know how he'd gotten callouses; he didn't shovel snow. They couldn't be from kneading chess men. It had to be the crutches. He clenched his stubbled jaw.

"Maybe. Until the next time."

His apparent sportsmanship surprised me, but I wasn't sure there would be a next time. Something was wrong. Had Franz been as focused as he should have been? I'd been so wound up for the match, it was only now I noticed two packed bags in one corner, one a bulging satchel made of telltale dimpled pigskin. It looked like it held contraband—maybe butter from a local farmer or something else to barter? They had tidied up their partition. But yellow newsprint remained wedged between their floor boards as the snow kept falling, muffling sounds inside the barracks.

Now I could hear Mother's voice in the distance, calling for me to get bread. She sounded plaintive, and I faintly smelled sliced onions. As always I'd enjoy the bakery, especially in the snow flurries. I was about to rise when Ludwig spoke, more words than he'd ever said. "Fact is there won't be a next time."

That startled me, though it confirmed my feeling.

"We're off to Australia. Know where Perth is? Off to a sheep ranch."

"You don't say? When?" I managed to say.

Perth lay on the other side of Australia, I thought I recalled from Fräulein Seebach's atlas. In fact it lay as far south and west as could be, lost in nowhere.

"The next transport," Ludwig said. "Along with a few others."

I wondered who. Most likely Sepp Blassmann and the Bobans.

Now Franz seemed to awaken. "The great outdoors," he sneered, back to his angry self. "It might interest you that we'll have more to do than play chess."

It was a sign he wouldn't be entirely gracious about his defeat.

"I'm a cook, you know, I cooked long before the war. Spitz's bean soup is slop, hardly enough to plug your gut. For the first time in a long time I'll have meat to cook. Mutton stew, for starters."

"A sheep ranch never lacks for work," said Ludwig, "and there's always work for handymen. Who else would hire us? I can carpenter on one leg, and one arm, for that matter."

I recalled his skill in those early days, when they'd built their partition. For the first time I saw how really bad his teeth were. Like Franz he suddenly extended his hand, a surprisingly fine-boned hand. Right then I was sure: Ludwig was the artist.

"Ludwig Janko," he introduced himself. "It's been a pleasure. Keep up the chess."

Again Mother called from deep within the barracks. Outside the cripples' grimy barracks window the snow sifted down, like flour dusting the foothills. I felt my throat clench. I looked around their penciled walls and lamely wished them luck.

"I always meant to ask," I dared. "Which one of you is the artist?"

Ludwig laughed—a cheerful rasp. "Whoever has the gift of sight. It could be me; it could be Franz. Only true perception matters."

I thought that meant Ludwig. That's what I wanted. It was Ludwig's little joke. He didn't want to show up Franz and liked to leave me guessing. For a second he made me think of Father.

Deep within the barracks, Mother called again.

I said, "I'd better go."

It was the last time I saw them. That evening Sepp Blassmann came by with Franjo Boban, Dubravka, and little Milan. Beetle-browed Milan looked stubbornly past me but hadn't been able to get out of stopping by with our noisy neighbors. Even in the refugee camp, it was basic courtesy. Father got out the schliwowitz he saved for special visitors, although the fragrant plum brandy came from a Serb. Franjo's eyes misted over even as Father extracted the bottle from behind the striped curtain above Mother's stove. The brandy reminded him of home. He raised his shot glass and closed his eyes.

"*Bože moj!*" he almost sobbed. "With friends like you, my God—"

Father wouldn't let him finish. "You're right, you hate to go. But how can you not?" He glanced at the somber Milan. "There's no escape; we need to find our futures. Here's to your land down under!"

Dubravka Boban put a protective arm around Milan. She was dark and handsome, a softer version of him. Milan seemed to wince but stood rigid like a fighter, too earnest now to be his father's little shit. Blassmann joined Franjo Boban in downing his plum brandy.

"To Australia," said Franjo, suddenly choked up with feeling.

Sepp stood mutely by until the Bobans had left, then shuffled awkwardly. "Our train's early tomorrow morning. From Salzburg north to Germany, then the long sea voyage." His laugh was hollow. "Hope someone's shoveled the snow off the tracks."

Father grinned. "Don't look to me," he said, choosing to make light of it. "With everyone deserting this stinking ship, the locals have to do their own dirty work."

Frowning, Mother disapproved of the joke and then looked at Sepp. "Isn't Mari coming to say goodbye?"

Sepp looked thunderstruck. I got the impression the Blassmanns' union hung by a thread, with the entire continent of Australia their last chance to save it.

"Mari's packing," he said, avoiding her eyes.

"It's a long trip, for sure," said Father. "You deserve a good early start."

"With all our hearts, we wish you both well," Mother said.

Father poured out one last toast. "Aren't Franz and Ludwig joining you?"

Mother's face lit up. The camp outcasts were leaving. No more naked female behinds. No more trying to figure out to where I'd disappeared or having to knock on their grimy door. Just as quickly, she seemed to scowl at Father. He should have told her that tomorrow was their departure day.

"Of course, they're going too," Sepp Blassmann muttered bleakly. Then he said, "You've been a true friend, Hans. I couldn't have asked for a better one."

Father said to write, to let us know how things were going. I didn't think it would happen. Sepp fumbled, misty-eyed, took Mother's hand, and looked at me without really seeing me. He gave Father a bear hug and was out the door.

CHAPTER 22

THE GOOD SHEPHERD

The Royalists were the next to go. They packed up after my big chess match. As a result our dreams suffered a detour that we couldn't refuse.

One of the departing Serbs found us a new home. The hulking Stjepan Šlajfer was an unlikely good shepherd. Born in a German-speaking farm town in the Vojvodina, Stjepan grew up a Serb in Belgrade, where his parents took him as a child. There they would have changed Schleifer to Šlajfer. But in Straubling he saw Father as a "countryman" who became his wary friend. His offer of a separate hut, Father saw right away, was an opportunity. We could gain a temporary shelter that would let us await America more calmly. Of course it would also put us right under old Fritz Krummbacher's nose, the switchman by the railroad tracks and Berti's father.

Father had already told me about the evening at Stubaier's where he first met Šlajfer. The drunken Stjepan stared at Bogdan Marković, a dashing Royalist comrade. As Bogdan whirled a peasant girl in a dance, his dark good looks irritated Šlajfer, who looked blond and German although he hardly spoke a word of it. The women favored Bogdan, dark mustache and all.

Just the same, when the Germans invaded Yugoslavia in 1941, both Stjepan and Bogdan became comrades—Royalist fighters linked to Mihailović, the Chetnik guerilla leader. But when the war ended, Tito's Communist partisans triumphed over the Germans and the Chetniks.

Stjepan and his comrades fled to Austria, where somehow they became special refugees. No black bean soup for them. He and his pals lived well and apparently without working. They had former German army housing right next to the American garrison, just as they once danced in the army warehouse that became our barracks. Their compound was light years from Lechner's pasture, where the Nazis had starved the Soviet POWs. Father wasn't sure who funded the Royalists. Maybe the Americans or the UN, just in case they could help topple Tito and restore the Yugoslav monarchy.

When Bogdan Marković finished dancing he brought the girl back with him. Stjepan put his large paws on their table and stared at Bogdan. Apropos nothing, he recited a Serbian ditty. Something about Bogdan's mother being a whore and his aunt and sister too, so that made three.

Some of the Serbs resumed dancing. Stjepan swigged his beer, then downed a schnapps. Mother and Father sat farther away with Florian Riedl, their friend the lumberjack. Next to his girlfriend, Vroni Gassinger, Florian looked like a sawed-off tree trunk from wrestling lumber sleds down snowy hillsides. A clutch of locals formed a wedge between the Serbs and the dance floor. Maybe needing rest due to their endless maneuvers, the American GIs were absent.

Handsome Bogdan moved as if in slow motion. Although they were friends, he raised his beer to smash Šlajfer across the face. Stjepan reached out and bounced his face to the table. The local girl fled, and their Serbian comrades rushed in to separate them. It took half a dozen to hold off Stjepan so he wouldn't kill Bogdan. The nervous innkeeper, Ludwig Stubaier, sent his boy off to call the gendarmes. He probably feared for his furniture. The younger Austrians competed with the Serbs for local girls. They looked primed to get their licks in but for now seemed content to let Šlajfer do their work. Father kept his distance until Stubaier sidled up to him, saying something about "your people."

This touched the old sore point with Father, who refused to consider Yugoslavia a country. For him it remained an unjust reward created by the victors of World War I for their Serb allies. He insisted its German speakers had come to the region when it was still part of Austria, although today's Austrians disdained us. With Stubaier whining, Father rose from his chair. Florian Riedl pulled him back.

"Ludwig, just shut up," he told the innkeeper. "This isn't our affair."

Stubaier tucked in his tail and left. The band launched into a brisk polka to lure guests to dance. It wasn't the first upheaval involving Stjepan,

Bogdan, and women. One chilly Sunday later, shortly after the chess players and Sepp Blassmann had left for down under, he came to see us. I saw him lumber from across the river and ran inside the barracks to tell Father. It looked like our time for visitors, even more than Sepp or Herr Gruber. Stjepan's head almost touched our low ceiling. He didn't seem embarrassed.

"Bogdan crows about his conquests," he said. "It gets to be too much."

"He's smooth," said Father. "And the girls like them dark and handsome."

"Or American, with deep pockets," Stjepan growled. His bloodshot eyes moved around our partition. "What a dump. Got anything to drink?" he asked before Father could offer.

Father shoved aside our dirty soup bowls, and Mother sent me outside to fetch fresh water to clean them. I hesitated. Something important would be discussed, and it was cold outside. As I struggled to tear myself away, Father pulled another clear bottle from the shelf over the stove behind its striped cloth, this time some of Austria's finest. He owed his stash of *enzian* to Florian, who seemed intent on making up for his stingy countrymen. Gavrilo Stepić, another of the Royalists, was the one who also sold Father the *schliwowitz.* Of course he called it *šjlivovica.*

Father poured. They spoke in Serbian. The barrack walls still had ears. The Bobans and Sepp Blassmann were off to Australia, but the snuffling next door sounded expectant. I heard Granny Pfeifer's bunk squeak. The next day she'd probably spread rumors about Father's being awash in schnapps and schliwowitz. Through our one window you could see dusk fall over the foothills. As Mother glared at me I finally hurried out. It had stopped snowing, but an icy cold descended as I tried pumping water from the well behind the soup kitchen. I broke the icicles off the spout, but still nothing came up. Finally I just scooped up clean snow to melt for water.

When I returned I waited outside our partition, hoping Mother wouldn't recall I was due with water. The wait was worth it. Stjepan Šlajfer's mood was foul, but he had an offer too good to refuse.

"Damned yodelers, all of them. To them we're just dirty interlopers."

We knew the feeling. *Zugroasti,* refugees.

Stjepan reached deep inside himself and spat out a gob of venom at Austria. "*Idi u pičku materinu!*" Something about "go to hell" or worse.

The snow was melting in my pan.

"Don't I know it," Father said mildly. "But Florian Riedl's all right."

"You're a countryman; that's why I stopped by. Can you get a strip of land, from him or anyone? I can get you a house to put on it."

Its ice floes clinking, the nearby Salzach flowed toward Salzburg. I heard it through our thin partition. Father leaned closer.

"We're dropping off the payroll," Stjepan growled, thumping his fists against his chest. "All of us stinking freeloaders."

Not waiting for Father to pour, he swigged from the bottle.

"Someone finally got wise. No more handouts, not even the Yanks are fooled. And goodbye, UN. My friend, the war's over; the monarchists are sloppy dead-enders. No one's taking on Tito; not even Stalin can budge him. It's every rat for himself, sliding down the nearest rope."

Šlajfer's words sounded ominous, but Father let him talk. He no longer tried to pour; they both drank from Florian's bottle.

"Time for Dragan, Rade, handsome Bogdan, me, and all the rest. Time to finally work. We're heading for Australia, Chile, and Canada—each to his own rat's nest. Stavrev and Janković even have relatives in Chicago. Whoever's willing to put us up until we learn to feed ourselves. Only Radić is staying; seems he may peddle life insurance. Can you believe it, with half of Europe croaking? Even Drazić is going, despite his local honey."

The names meant nothing to me as I listened outside. Father probably knew them. What mattered was Stjepan and what he might have to offer.

"The new world's recast in iron," added Stjepan and swigged from the bottle. "End of illusions, end of war."

"Churchill's Iron Curtain," Father mused. "And where will you be going?"

"My father's sister in Melbourne. If she's still kicking, I'll find this auntie Katica. Else I'm off to Canada—some cousins of Popović are farming north of Toronto. Once they see how much I eat, they'll hate me soon enough."

Father laughed and toasted him. *"Nazdravlje."*

Stjepan got to the heart of things. "Remember little Gavrilo?"

Of course Father knew Gavrilo Stepić. "Fine *šjlivovica.*"

"The slippery runt who runs our camp store," Šlajfer said anyway, "the one his father named after the great hero, Gavrilo Princip. Can't say it got him immortality. The same runt who chisels us each payday on his *šjlivovica*, or should I say, the day of dole? Once we pull up our garrison, Gavrilo's little shack is up for grabs. The one with that little vendor's window. Unless someone were to buy it."

The snow in my tin pan had finished melting.

Father leaned in. "How much?"

CHAPTER 23

"ŽIVELI!"

The shack must have been a bargain, although I couldn't quite hear the price. A month later, Father raised the little hut on a patch of land north of the camp between the train tracks and the Salzach River. Florian Riedl loaned him the purchase price, helped him dismantle the little vendor's shack, got him a strip of land—Lechner owed him for lumber—and pitched in with his cart and horses to raise the hut. I helped them guide the beams and boards as they pulled them off the wagon. While they raised the hut with ropes and arms, I tried to stabilize the lumber. As they hammered that wet spring, I pounded straight their crooked nails. Father already envisioned more—a chicken coop and Mother's laundry shed.

Even though some refugees had already left, we got out of the camp with its stink and gossip. Like Berti, I now got a clear view across the river toward the American army dump ground as the trucks pulled up, even though I wasn't supposed to prospect. But now we lived just under the nose of old Fritz Krummbacher and my classmate Berti, who still liked to play the big shot, and we depended on their well for water. The creek to our left was usually dry, with barely water to scrub dishes. But old Fritz already warned us it could turn savage during heavy rains.

"It's a wild water. Could sweep your shack with it."

"Let's hope not," Father said with a shrug. But later I saw him by the dry creek bed studying its stones. It hardly looked violent, but I guessed you never knew.

We saw Stjepan Šlajfer one more time that soggy spring. He trudged to our new hut and rocked the floor boards as he entered. I was outside admiring our new chicken coop; Mother sold fresh eggs, and her prize Leghorn, Granny, was her most prolific layer. I wiped my hands on my sleeves and looked inside the hut.

Father had Stjepan sit down and was about to offer him more of Florian's schnapps with that tang of herbs, then recalled the schliwowitz stashed behind the cabbage barrel. It was a bottle Gavrilo Stepić had thrown in to seal their bargain on the hut. Father laughed; so did Šlajfer. He probably got some bottles too, for brokering the deal. Both chose the schliwowitz, their native plum brandy. It was good they sat down.

At over two meters tall, Šlajfer's curly blond head again almost touched our ceiling. He looked menacing. In my grand scheme of men you could trust or couldn't, I wasn't quite sure where Stjepan fit. I'd begun to add a third rule—Father's "never get too comfortable." But with America on my brain, I thought that just possibly Stjepan Šlajfer could take on Jersey Joe if he could grab him in a bear hug and stop Joe's hammering fists. As though christening our new home, this time Father poured.

Stjepan said he'd chosen Canada with Popović at his cousins' farm. Eventually, he thought, he'd find work in Toronto, once he knew some English. He might even work his way farther south to Detroit or Chicago. He hadn't found his aunt in Melbourne.

"It's just as well," he said. "I'm not fit to keep her company. But if you ever get a chance, look me up. I'll send you my address."

As he drank he looked around our new home—Gavrilo's tiny vendor shack of two small rooms, one a kitchen, and a living area holding a big bed and table. Mother had put up print curtains, and Stjepan looked surprised, as if seeing it with new eyes. She already used Gavrilo's little window to call outside whenever she wanted me for errands. For sure she wasn't selling spirits. With her constant calls and chores, she didn't give me much time to read even when I had material. Mostly I got her pails of clean water to feed her hungry laundry shed. Unfortunately that meant using old Krummbacher's well more often than I liked. But she washed GI uniforms and they first needed soaking. Right now she had the little window open for air; it made me recall the Royalists' farewell party.

The tiny hut with Šlajfer and Father in it had recently been crammed with noisy, drinking Serbs. Many of us boys, locals and refugees, hovered outside. I saw Norbert and even Berti. Suddenly someone's hand, I think

Gavrilo's, reached through the little window and threw out a fistful of change. We plunged, then I saw the coins were pale *groschen*. With the Austrian schilling a pittance to the American dollar and a hundred groschen to one schilling, I let the others scramble. As Father said, a little dignity never hurt. I let Berti dive for his tarnished Austrian pennies. Looking around our new home, Šlajfer recalled the celebration.

"Your kid was there too, looking skeptical," he added, laughing.

Father saw me in the doorway. "Kept your nose clean?"

I didn't like his question.

"Come on, everyone likes a little celebration," said Stjepan. He shook my hand in his big paw as I edged closer and raised his shot glass to both of us. "*Živeli!*"

Father raised his. "To your health!"

Stjepan had no use for somber sentiments and kept his goodbye short. When he rose, his frame darkened our doorway and the hut looked even tinier.

"Enjoy your new home. Just don't get stuck in this rathole."

"*Ja se nedam!*" Father said. "Never say die." He must have told Stjepan about our plans for America.

As the swollen Salzach rolled past, Stjepan Šlajfer laughed and went his way.

CHAPTER 24

THE GUARD

One day after school, near Luise Gstaltmeier's, I ran into Herr Gruber. Maybe her Golden Jug offered him more hospitality than she'd shown me the last summer. The emperor still roomed at his inn, Zum Hirschen, down by the south bridge, while doing odd jobs and drawing his small pension. I'd last seen him one evening with a lilt in his gait. Spring had turned brisk, and the chill made me want to hurry home. But the emperor appeared in good spirits, if a little awkward.

"And how is school, young man?"

It was a change from "little man," but with his usual gentle courtesy.

"Good afternoon, Herr Gruber," I said. As always I liked the emperor, if not some other adults. "I like school."

"Your father says you're doing well. Quite well, in fact." He searched for things to say, yet his words were the first time I'd actually gotten Father's opinion on my studies. His pride seemed to spill over to Herr Gruber but not to me directly; maybe he didn't want to spoil me. Herr Gruber, in the meantime, checked out my dark green American coat with its zippered hood, a donation from the previous spring. It made me recall the little American girl who wanted to kill Germans and screamed at me through her compound's fence. Did the coat prompt her jealous rage?

"Your coat suits you," said the emperor. "You already look American."

"It's from a distribution. I managed to retrieve it."

I liked the padded coat, the warm lined hood especially. You could even lie down in a snowbank without getting snow down your neck. I didn't mention the pious Simon Dachnagl, who liked to supervise the camp distributions.

Herr Gruber looked grateful I had spoken. "Yes, yes, I must have left the camp before that." He didn't mention his drinking or his awkward departure.

I offered, "It keeps me warm in cold weather."

"Excellent, young man. You deserve it."

I could see he was running out of things to say.

"Yes," he concluded, "it's always good to see you. And say hello for me to your mother and father, young man. Tell them I'll stop by."

The emperor returned his pipe below his mustache and walked back toward his inn. Suddenly, as I watched him, out of the corner of my eye I glimpsed someone else. A uniformed American with a pencil mustache bowed smartly to none other than my teacher, Inge Seebach. As he doffed his visored cap, I saw he'd managed to part his cropped hair exactly as described by Herbert Mautner—cleanly down the middle. I'd never seen hair parted that way.

My teacher's special friend was full of surprises. The American would have to be the major Herbert knew as Curtis Bishop from the state of Texas. Despite his rank and decorations, it was a very proper encounter, unlike those Father ascribed to soldiers and especially to the Royalists. I sniffed the wintry April cold. Unaware of me, my teacher and the major entered Meindl's coffee store, with its aroma of roasted beans. Real coffee, not ersatz beans.

I didn't know of anyone who could afford them. I didn't want to stare and pretended to follow the receding emperor with my eyes. Under the raw April sky, his puffs of pipe smoke hung like chalk dust in the air.

That evening I mentioned the emperor's greeting but not the major. Father wryly attributed Herr Gruber's good spirits to his living "right above the tap." At first I couldn't tell if he meant to be cruel or felt a rueful sympathy.

"For shame, Hans," Mother said.

"He was coming from The Golden Jug," I said naively.

Father winked at Mother.

As if he'd heard us, two days later the emperor came to visit and admired our new premises. Mother probably knitted so she wouldn't have to say much. Maybe she felt awkward about how she'd once seen Herr Gruber. You could see he no longer looked quite the emperor. He looked tired and melancholy, his recent good spirits spent. His suit was wrinkled, his eyes were cloudy, and his green lapels were flecked with food stains. Dark half-moons of dirt showed under his nails, and his yellowing mustache drooped. He kept his coat on. Our small hut looked friendlier than our old cubicle but was only slightly warmer inside than the chill spring outside.

"Indeed," Herr Gruber said. "How times have changed, Herr Kemper. I remember my estate, my rolling pastures in Bohemia's countryside. Lord of my domain. And in the evenings, comradeship at the inn. The way things used to be."

Father voice was low. "And how's the lady?"

Herr Gruber flushed, now even less the emperor. "Ups and downs; yes, ups and downs." Again he found his memories. "Ah, those rolling fields. People here will never know. They're small; they think small. If only she could see them."

I didn't know who "she" was.

"People just aren't how they once were. The Czechs hated us Sudeten Germans. Today's Austria despises us refugees, even though our blood's German too. Although once we all lived in Austria-Hungary, our empire, as brothers. You're right to plan for America. My own daughter doesn't want me. Mind you, Erna was always her mother's girl. Even though I'd bring her pralines from Pilsen and rocked her on my knee. Yes, the gallant old Austria-Hungary is no more. You should have seen our spirit, the valor of our troops in the *K.u.K.* We threw ourselves into the fray! It took all of giant Russia, its brutish mass of men, to nudge the Eastern front even three centimeters past the Carpathians! And for what, Herr Kemper? The Great War lost, the emperor dead, everything splendid lost."

Herr Gruber's words trailed off.

"Versailles," Father agreed, "created a new world and opened a box of horrors."

For some reason, a little later I told Father about Fräulein Seebach and her American major. Hours after our lunch at school I could still feel the mash of polenta lodged deep in my gut. In part it was due to the major, pencil mustache and all.

"It's not our business," Father chided me. "Anyway, your teacher's a fine lady."

"I think it's where she gets those tissues."

"And what else, nylons? But what are these tissues?"

I must have sounded comical. "Paper handkerchiefs to blow your nose."

"The things you stick your nose in, Konrad," Father said with a laugh, turning the tables. "You're insatiable. Good thing she likes you. Isn't it time for your homework?"

It was, and I had almost finished, but the next day after school I couldn't resist my urge to prospect. Indulging my curiosity about America just one more time, I poked and puttered and eventually came across some documents buried deep within the dump. I hesitated to tell Father. I wasn't supposed to prospect. And I couldn't read the English, but the papers looked important. In fact so important that I wondered whether Fräulein Seebach's American major might have handled them. He seemed to be everywhere. After all, Herbert Mautner knew about him; he might have been the army's liaison to the court.

I was sure about one thing, though. The mug shots on the first page, front view and profile, showed a man with a sharp nose and dark mustache, Alois Lechner's spitting image. In spite of everything, I thought I'd better tell Father. There might be something in the photos for us, or something Lechner needed. By the petroleum lamp in our new hut, Father studied them.

"Where did you find these?" he said sternly.

I managed to get the words out.

"So you went prospecting anyway?" he said. "After what I told you?"

"I couldn't resist," I squirmed.

Father stared at me for the longest time, subdued but angry. Suddenly he slapped me, but not as hard as he could have. I saw stars anyway. "Then you know what that was for," he said.

I remembered his reaction when Franjo Boban punished little Milan. Now I was his little shit and yet his pride and joy. "Never again," I promised.

He spread the mug shots on our table. "It's Lechner, all right. From the American army dump ground, did you say?"

I nodded, my cheek burning. Having found the papers, I felt I'd earned the right to ask, "What do you suppose they mean?"

"You did one thing right," Father said; "you brought me these papers. But first, not a word to anyone. Whatever happened in the war, it's over. And whatever these papers mean now, they've been thrown out. So maybe they no longer matter."

I was anxious to hear the rest.

"Just the same," concluded Father, "we all know about the prison camp. You've seen the site, I'm sure. They set it up on Lechner's land; it's probably why the Americans had a file on him. I assume none of it was his fault, and the investigation's over. But just to let him know, I'll take him these papers." His sudden wink was knowing. "We have his interest at heart, don't we?"

Again I nodded. Lechner should know he owed us a favor.

Later Father told me Alois Lechner's reaction when he took him the dossier. His voice rose in outrage. He squirmed at the indignity, both at the photos and at Father's knowing—a mere refugee knowing—and even having to be grateful.

"It's the height of arrogance. The Americans tear up my fields on maneuvers. I can't plan, can't till, can't sow. All I can do is graze a few head of cows between times. And all the time, they act like I'm the criminal. Even compile a secret dossier!"

"The Russian prisoners?" Father said mildly, although he knew the answer.

"Those sorry bastards, of course. That must be it. As if I had anything at all to do with that! The Wehrmacht just took over. Took my best fields for their dirty camp."

"Flat terrain, easy to watch, and beyond the river's bend. From their point of view, I guess it all made sense," Father mused. "No doubt a good and private place, and the river masked all sounds." He looked hard at Alois Lechner. "Did they offer you cheap labor, down there in your fields?"

Lechner blanched. Whose side are you on, his face seemed to plead. "I couldn't win no matter what. They just took my fields. And now it's the Americans!"

"You're burdened with a prize," said Father dryly, "prime bottom land. I know; I used to farm. You want to till your land. But Austria's occupied territory."

Lechner wiped his brow. "I'm no Otto Jabuka, or even his shiftless brother. He's been skulking around, as if Otto hadn't done enough. I hardly knew him or even his brother now. He probably enjoyed taking shovels to prisoners' skulls."

Jabuka had one of those obscure names that seemed to abound in all corners of Central Europe once ruled by Austria-Hungary. I didn't know much about him except what I'd learned from Herbert Mautner. And whoever he was, I hadn't met his brother.

"Be glad you weren't a guard like him," Father said. "He'll be forever damned."

Lechner wouldn't look at him. Whatever he felt, he didn't want to be chums with him—Father already knew too much—or be chummy with any refugee. But a few weeks later he returned the favor. Father had almost forgotten about it when one of Lechner's farmhands pulled a heavy cart up to our vegetable patch and dumped a load of steaming steer manure. It was a visit as productive as unannounced. A farmer in his previous life, Father sniffed the air.

"Go tell your mother. Come June we'll be in carrots, cabbages, and tomatoes. The gods are good to us."

CHAPTER 25

THE AMERICAN COAT

Despite the way I got it, I liked the coat admired by the emperor. It brought me closer to America, which I was still discovering, and shielded me from snow and cold gusts in the spring. But the American coat also reminded me of Simon Dachnagl, our weekly instructor in religion hour. I recalled the distribution day the previous spring, before the exodus had begun.

Our barracks roof leaked from melting snow. The whole gang was up and chattering—Norbert Pfeifer, little Jiři Kratky, his playmate Hedwig Hutz, and her snot-nosed sister, Gerda, who never wore underpants. Nearby hovered the camp women, "Genghis Khan" Vera Kratky, rail-thin Hutz, and Granny Pfeifer, her mouth as usual moving, along with all the others, except I think the floozy. Margit had other sources.

Even the childless refugees looked on, anxious or superior, including Spitz, our slimy cook. Soon they did more than watch; they dug into the spoils. Only two inmates were missing, the chess players Franz and Ludwig. Was it pride, or just too hard to balance on one leg while digging through clothes? You had to stoop to have a chance.

Behind everyone towered Gustav Finger, our camp supervisor, like a morbid oak. Beside him beamed the benevolent Dachnagl, while the snow melted in the foothills beyond them. In his billowing green *loden* coat, Dachnagl watched his shabby flock. His jowls gleamed like his fleshy lips. I didn't like his oily face, and I think neither did Father.

It was a distribution day—a donation of used clothes and shoes.

From America, said some. CARE packages, claimed others. Even the UN was cited as the source. The competition promised to be ugly, but I hoped the source was America. It would offer quality. Father sent me off to rummage, even if it resembled prospecting. It made it easier when he winked at me, with a glance at Simon Dachnagl.

"Good things," he said with a chuckle, "generally come from above."

"You mean America?" chimed in Spitz. "Canada's good enough for me!"

"Shut up, piss pot," old Stipe Baumann cursed in Croatian. He looked scornfully toward Gustav Finger, the camp supervisor who posed nobly, his arms across his chest. We assumed he'd gotten first take right off the top, to keep or barter, when the bounty was delivered.

Mother egged me on, and Father added, "Go get 'em, Konrad!"

On my knees, I groped through a mound of shoes but found the laces tangled. I wanted sturdy walking shoes, and then I found a boot. Fishing for its match, I pulled out one, then others, but none paired with the boot. As I stooped at mound level, a muddy shoe stepped on my hands. Enraged, I looked up to see Toni Spitz. He wore his tie as always, not caring where he stepped.

With no quick result, I gave up on the shoe pile. I'd have to move quickly elsewhere before all prizes were scooped up. Now I found the green padded coat with the handy hood. Right away I saw it let you lie in wet leaves or even snow, since the zippered hood circled your neck. In fact once I wore it, a woman uptown asked me, "Are you American?" The green coat no doubt helped propel me toward America. Luckily I got it one size too large, because over the next year it tightened. That encouraged me about the growth spurt. It meant I wasn't shrinking.

Meanwhile, back at the shoe pile, Wilma Hutz and Granny Pfeifer both latched onto uneven pairs of dainty pumps. Between the two of them, they could have traded for two perfect pairs but instead chose to bicker.

As the clouds scudded toward the snow-patched foothills and the raw Salzach rushed north, Simon Dachnagl chose this moment to lead us in prayer. Attended by Finger, he doffed his felt hat to expose his naked skull.

"Dear friends," he began, "we have not been abandoned."

Our diggers barely looked up, unwilling to stop mining. Before speaking Dachnagl had worked his way, counseling parents and noting any mischief, especially some boys' short attention spans during religion hour. Just behind him Gustav Finger wore what looked like a fashionable American coat, probably scooped right off the top.

"No, we have not been abandoned," repeated Dachnagl. In my mind, as he praised God and our benefactors, I added his name to those you couldn't trust. The day went downhill from there, but I had my green coat. Even Dachnagl noticed when no one paid him attention. He crossed himself and bowed his head.

Now, one year later, we had our new quarters—the hut in which to await America. With Dachnagl away on parish business, one day a substitute filled in at our religion class. In that one hour, Klaus Sekyra won us over. Like Vera Kratky, he was a refugee from Bohemia, but in his case that made me trust him. To end the hour he told a tale that left us awed. Even Berti Krummbacher perked up when Sekyra told about a greater switchman. It was a haunting tale that matched the drama of the church. As Klaus Sekyra told it, a train rushed through the night.

Beyond the luminous cone cast by its headlamp, the engineer looked up to see a shadow wave its arms. Just a vague shadow, but aflicker in alarm. The train rushed on full throttle, its wheels champing as rain fell like needles through the light. And again the engineer saw the shadow, someone waving his arms to signal him to stop. He knew it wasn't a switchman; the station lay too far. But again the shadow flickered before the hurtling train. And the engineer began to wonder, what if—and what then? If it wasn't the switchman, could it be someone else?

"Did he stop?" asked Susi Palfner, who still disliked foreigners.

"Yes, he finally stopped," said Klaus Sekyra, as even gossipy Berti hushed.

"It wasn't the switchman, was it?" piped up Gustl Ponkratz.

"A greater switchman, by far. And remember, children, he works in mysterious ways."

The uneasy engineer finally did stop and found no one, but still the shadow waved its arms. It signaled to some rhythm and recurred in the light. He found a fly trapped behind the lens, beating its wings before the lamp. And the bridge two hundred meters on, washed out by the storm.

We sighed like air leaving a balloon. Berti turned away, working not to show awe.

CHAPTER 26

THIEVES AND LIARS

The next Sunday after Mass, I sought out Klaus Sekyra at the rectory. Straubling had no public library; it was the only place to borrow books. I hadn't remotely quenched my thirst with *The Master of Ballantrae*. Despite Father's urging, trying to read *The Master* in English was impossible, even to prepare me for America. And in my schoolbooks no one was ever killed or even robbed.

But it had turned out to be a struggle to get anything juicy at the rectory. The priests had rules. They only lent out books "not unwholesome for a tender mind," as they once told Mother. Even Klaus Sekyra couldn't break those rules, not as an assistant priest. Those rules were the monsignor's—the steady Andreas Bruck. No love stories, deep philosophy, and never death or murder. They might cause unhealthy fantasies. So I slogged through what I got, like the troops through Lechner's mud.

Until sometimes, by accident, a lurid volume got by the priests. Once Klaus Sekyra gave me something on the bloody intrigue during the French Revolution. The Jacobins made heads roll until their own heads bounced. Primed, one Sunday I was desperate enough to dare Sekyra to relent.

"I love to read," I said earnestly, "and I can handle real adventure. Do you have any books about America?"

Sekyra shook his head. "Are you sure you're ready for the Wild West?"

That encouraged me; he saw what I wanted. "For a long time," I said.

He smiled. "How old are you exactly, Konrad?"

Always that question. "Soon I'll be twelve," I said, exaggerating.

"Adventure tales are meant for the older boys. Normally that means fourteen."

I waited silently. He seemed struck by my determination.

"But I suppose for you," he finally said, "we'll just have to make an exception. Keep in mind, these aren't life; they're stories."

From then on I always looked for Klaus Sekyra to be on duty Sunday mornings. He began giving me Karl May adventure tales set in the Orient or west of the Mississippi. They were anything but regular stories. I began to ride alongside Hadji Halef Omar and Kara Ben Nemsi Effendi, even on Mecca pilgrimages at risk to my life and Christian soul, and with them tracked an evil saint across Oriental desert sands. Above all I roamed the farthest West.

I journeyed on Mississippi river boats and watched my back, thirsted in Death Valley with intrepid heroes, was betrayed by a saddle tramp to raiding Kiowa, and joined Apache councils. I ached to be a noble redskin and despised the lying palefaces. Father approved my zest for reading as long as good men won and even gave me coins to borrow more books. I didn't even tell Herbert Mautner, but Berti found out by accident.

"Karl May's a windbag," he sneered. "I doubt he ever saw an Indian."

"*Ruh lil dschehennem,*" I told him, using a phrase from May's Oriental travels. "Go to hell."

"That just shows you. He got that scrap from a dictionary. He didn't know a word of Arabic."

He was trying to turn the tables, as I'd done with Norbert over distance vision.

"May had to invent," I said. "All writers do. But he starts with basic facts."

"He was a liar and a con man—even got jailed for petty theft. It's a good thing he started writing so he could make his money by lying."

I was stronger and took after him. Poised for my growth spurt, I had a wiry energy. My chores for Father probably helped. Berti leaped from our shack toward his father's gate by their yellow switchman's house.

"Balkan scum," he yelped. "Watch us cut off your water. No more slopping at our well!"

I wanted to pummel him but held back. Father wouldn't like it. We were on sufferance on our patch of land, squeezed between the river and the railroad tracks. Without drinking water we were nothing. Fortunately, two days later Father brought home a book that soothed my frustration. It was like an explosion. On a construction job in attic space below a broken roof, he'd salvaged the dusty novel. Printed in Gothic font, it had the force of truth. Even its paper was more durable than books printed since the war. Karl May was just a charlatan next to *Die Regulatoren in Arkansas*. Its author had spent years in America and knew the splendors of the West.

On the very first page of *The Regulators* a storm raged through a forest clearing. A cunning Methodist preacher, Rowson, met with his pack of outlaws. His preaching masked a life of crime. After many ups and downs, in the end his mask was ripped off. *The Regulators in Arkansas* left me elated with its bloody treachery and its savage storms and landscapes. As if to please Father, law and order mostly triumphed, and the vigilantes got their man.

Simon Dachnagl, in the meantime, never loaned me one book about America although he claimed to support us refugees. Before we left for America, he'd strut through the camp as the women clucked. It was usually the women he sought out on his shepherd rounds. Wilma Hutz would flutter, leading to unsavory gossip. He blessed everyone he met and prodded us boys to master the Act of Contrition. To our credit, most of us stumbled. As hawk-eyed Granny Pfeifer watched, even Norbert dared to fail. I began to see him with new eyes, while Dachnagl's eyes narrowed at his charade. One day after we'd moved to our new hut, something outraged him openly.

A dozen Volga German refugees, women and children from much farther east, had arrived from Salzburg and temporarily joined our camp. They spoke their German with Russian accents, including Leonid, a hulking boy in smelly rags. One day Leonid supposedly broke into the church poor box. I was never sure whether he'd been caught at it or whether a local had seen him flush with coins and jumped to conclusions. But Simon Dachnagl seemed to take it personally.

The next day, in religion hour, he cross-examined Leonid in front of everyone. A whiff of quark still lingered, an ancient souvenir from the cheese that Gustl Ponkratz had once dropped into the coils of the radiator. The smell competed with Leonid's, who whimpered in broken German.

"*Ich nicht tun! Es war anderer.*"

Simon Dachnagl slapped him. "Liar!"

"Was someone else, not me," sobbed Leonid.

Dachnagl struck him harder. The blow was savage, much worse than Franjo Boban punishing little Milan. For every denial from Leonid, Dachnagl whacked his blubbering face. Finally blood streamed from his nose, and it wasn't clear who was more exhausted, Leonid or the priest.

Our class watched, stunned yet fascinated, relieved we weren't being punished. Only Monika Waldegger, the pretty one, and Herbert Mautner seemed unafraid. Herbert looked in my direction and ever so slightly rolled his eyes. I looked uneasily at Gustl Ponkratz, whom I'd once given that bloody nose. But the gossipy Berti seemed eager, as though the incident confirmed all his suspicions about refugees. I'd be hearing more from him.

Now Dachnagl wiped his sweaty face and turned, as if to check our stunned reaction to the example he'd made of Leonid. He looked satisfied by what he saw and marched Leonid outside. Soon Fräulein Seebach returned, strangely quiet, to resume our regular instruction. We never saw Leonid again.

At day's end, not quite sure why, I left school somber and defiant.

CHAPTER 27

THE BUILDERS

All this time, Father immersed me in work at our new hut. After school I chopped wood, helped build the laundry shed, carried water for Mother's laundering, and scraped out the chicken coop. I wrote these tasks off to experience. To succeed in America, Father said, immigrants had to give 200 percent. I was training for America just as Jersey Joe trained for Charles. But we faced detours, in a way just more training.

As I toiled I began to notice activity on nearby land. One afternoon, as Father and I worked more of Lechner's steer manure into our vegetable plot, a man strode toward us from next door. His walk was stately, like a stork's. He seemed to balance briefly on each leg as he raised the other for his next step and he carried a roll of blue paper under one arm. He sniffed the steer manure. We sniffed right back. Something about him promised money.

He almost clicked his muddy boots. "Kurt Pfeil."

"Hans Kemper," Father answered. He seemed to know Pfeil, a refugee from Soviet-occupied Vienna and, someone said, a former SS colonel. Inspecting the terrain he'd just acquired, Pfeil had seen us dig.

"What are you planting?" he asked.

"Whatever grows," said Father, "tomatoes, string beans, potatoes. I expect a good crop. The climate's cool and moist; the soil's almost virgin. Probably hasn't been turned since before the war."

Pfeil glanced over our plot and then toward a rusting German jeep left by the war. Its camouflage-green-and-tan hull lay half suspended over the creek bed. His blue eyes narrowed.

"The war put things on hold. It's good to see you dig. I have an instinct, about men it's unerring."

So did Father. "What was your front?"

"*Afrika Korps.* The Desert Fox."

"Hotter than hell down there, I've heard."

"Rommel gave them hell," corrected Pfeil. Even under Straubling's cloudy skies he looked tanned. "Do you want to make some money?"

"Of course," Father said. We needed clothes, needed shoes, and now we had Gavrilo's little hut to pay off. "What do you have in mind?"

Pfeil had in mind a driver training school for Straubling. It was a daring plan, since only prewar trucks with cranks and hood flaps now stuttered over gravel roads. The only passenger car belonged to Gustl's father, the mayor Anton Ponkratz. Pfeil already had his blueprints—the roll of paper—and would soon start his foundation. He planned to build with concrete blocks, a new procedure. He had lumber, cement, and gravel, for making block-size wooden molds and the mortar they would hold and shape. Pfeil already had one helper, a Slovenian refugee.

"That's where you would come in," he told Father. "You're a worker too."

"So you don't trust your fellow Austrians?"

"Exactly," Pfeil said and laughed. "You refugees are hungrier. It's all about a vision, in peace as in war. Just you wait a few years. Before you know it, cars will fill up Straubling. It'll take a Viennese like me to show the locals on which side their bread is buttered. Straubling's virgin, like your garden. My builder's Georg Seidl; he's from Vienna too. Despite that recent film, the city's still our heart and soul."

Pfeil must have meant *The Third Man*. He slapped his blueprint.

"I have *Baumeister* Seidl's plans right here. He'll do it for less to get in, and I'd like to throw him some business."

I could tell Father liked what he heard. It sounded like another detour in our plans for America, but like our new hut, one we couldn't refuse. Our finances would perk up, and that by working right next door. Success might lead to more success, and it would prime us for America. Just because we had plans, we couldn't rust waiting. And though he dreamed of Australia, the Slovenian was another positive omen. France Pregelj had a talent for friendship and worked hard. He already knew those who, like Franjo Boban, had already sailed for the land down under.

Father and France made a good team. They alternated filling molds for building blocks with digging Pfeil's foundation. Soon bullet-headed Georg Seidl, the builder, came to inspect their work. Like Toni Spitz, our former cook, Seidl liked his shirt white with a black tie, and he had Dachnagl's fleshy lips. Right off I disliked him. One day, as I weeded among our bean and cabbage sprouts, I saw him with Kurt Pfeil. Their conversation looked important.

Father had taken a break, and I smelled Mother's cooking in our hut; I thought I knew what. She still mourned the death of Granny, her favorite Leghorn. That familiar gravel truck had run over the hen out on the road before Mother's eyes, then the driver leaned out his cab to stutter an apology. He was friends with Florian Riedl, and we hadn't seen the last of him. Still, you couldn't let Granny go to waste.

I inhaled the kitchen aroma just as Georg Seidl started toward me. In a generous tone, he asked to speak with Father. Soon he introduced himself to Father.

"*Georg Seidl, habe die Ehre.* It's a pleasure watching you work. You're organized and thorough; I can use a man like you."

Father studied him coolly. Just as we made our plans for America, suddenly job prospects bloomed everywhere. "What do you have in mind?" he asked once again.

"I believe Pfeil's told you I'm his builder. My firm needs good workers."

Father mentioned a local rival. "Competition would be good for Taxenbacher."

Seidl straightened his black tie. "I like your attitude. Old Taxenbacher wants to squeeze me out. But I'm an architect; I'm not just some interloper."

Father laughed; he knew the locals. "A two-edged sword, Herr Seidl."

"Indeed." Seidl looked vexed. "Pfeil said you weren't prone to undue reverence. I don't mind, as long as you're a steady worker."

Father saw our funds deepening as we waited to emigrate. He ignored Seidl's patter. "When do I start?"

"Excellent! As soon as Pfeil's trenches for the foundation and the building blocks are ready. You'll be working with old Mittermeier, he knows the trade. It's a golden opportunity to learn while you get paid."

Father winked at me. "Exactly my thinking."

They shook on the deal. Seidl rejoined Pfeil to finish their important discussion.

"Could Mother be cooking rabbit?" I asked Father, feigning ignorance. "Or is it fowl?"

As so often, Father called me a strizi, a city slicker. "Let's go discover, Konrad."

It was savory fowl all right—Mother's prolific layer, Granny. Mother had outdone herself. I almost laughed at her next words but then noticed her disgust.

"When this fancy driving school opens," she snorted, "sign that fool up for lessons." She was talking about the driver, Florian Riedl's friend. "After what I went through, has my stew ever been better?"

We quickly agreed. After our fragrant goulash, Father rejoined France Pregelj. "The *strizi* wants to hire me." He meant Seidl. "Do you want in?"

"I'm sorry, Hans," France apologized, "but this foundation could be my last. I've got one foot in Australia." He looked dejected but then named others destined for Australia. "We'll take the same train to Salzburg. A mixed crew, but it's a start."

"I hate to see you go," said Father, "but no one deserves a good start more. But when you do, at least kick Spitz and Finger for me. Hard."

As they laughed, I looked forward to the coming farewell celebration. Mother would cook something special, maybe more goulash with the fresh vegetables I tended. Or Florian Riedl might bring down some mountain goat, *gams* he poached high above on Lechner's Alpine range. In the meantime, to his delight, Seidl saw his view of Father's work confirmed. He even began to share his sorrows.

As he studied the rising walls of Pfeil's driver training school, he sometimes caught his hired hands loafing and would lapse into a singsong. "Don't think, Herr Kemper, I don't see the shirking. I see everything. And it gnaws at me. But I say nothing, not a word."

Father would check his amusement as Seidl gestured skyward, as if to berate the gods. But he would chuckle afterward. In fact he learned quickly, although he'd begun as a helper. Georg Seidl's fledgling firm taught him to mix mortar, throw wet stucco over bricks, and, hardest of all, to lay straight rows of bricks himself.

When Sepp Mittermeier, his old teacher, left Seidl's pomp and wages for the firm of Taxenbacher, Father asked to take over. Bricklaying paid better than shoveling snow and wasn't as dangerous as logging, judging by Florian Riedl's stories. And it was steady work, unlike the seasonal snow-clearing or logging. Austria had begun to repair war damage and rundown buildings. Seidl was desperate for a bricklayer and leaped at Father's interest but hedged at paying bricklayer's wages.

"Let's first see how it works out. You're just learning the trade."

"There's nothing to it," Father said.

"Ah, but there's much more," said Seidl.

"All right, let's give it a try," Father said.

But he already had his sights set elsewhere. On weekends he'd developed a clientele for black market jobs too small for even Seidl or his rival Taxenbacher—jobs where he paid no taxes but which paid cash straight into his pocket. These were jobs such as patching the corner of a barn sheared off by a manure cart, freshening the stucco outside Stubaier's pantry, or patching a leak in Greiff's wine cellar, whose father Herbert Mautner and I had seen laid out. Father became known for discreet, solid work. Sometimes there was a bonus. Whenever he worked for Greiff, as I said, he and the merchant's Tyrolese assistant would thread a hose into a cask to enjoy their lunch with wine.

Things in Austria began to look promising, maybe too much so. Unexpectedly, Mother again chose to fight America. Father told me not to worry; it was probably all the uncertainty.

"And who can blame her? She fears the unknown." Suddenly he grinned. "You might say Austria's getting too comfortable, like a dirty old shoe. She needs to be more involved. Would you want to leave all the big decisions for the likes of you and me?"

I had to laugh. Mother still cleaned mornings at Dr. Wolfgang Deutlinger's, another refugee from Soviet Vienna. But by now she tripled that income weekends doing laundry for American soldiers. As the one who fetched the water for her hungry laundry shed, I knew. And by the time the beans and cabbages sprouted, she saw no reason to leave Austria.

"Pull yourself together," Father finally scolded. "We're still second class here."

"They trust you with their barns and cellars," she countered.

"Enlightened self-interest. Think of Konrad's education," he said.

That silenced her temporarily. He even promised her that cuckoo clock.

In the meantime Georg Seidl's fortunes declined. In Straubling he remained an interloper, highly trained but swimming upstream. Trying to build in the shadow of Taxenbacher, he found that being Viennese hurt. The locals didn't trust the city slickers. Since he'd also fled Vienna's Soviet zone, they spread rumors he'd belonged to the party. It was shorthand for the Nazis. Maybe he'd been only a minor functionary, but some also wanted to shift the focus away from their own past.

With his bricklayer's wages still unpaid, Father said, "Then it's settled, Herr Seidl."

Seidl looked up anxiously. "Settled? What do you mean?"

"I'll be seeking other employment."

Georg Seidl licked his fleshy lips. "What? My firm took you in. I taught you the trade."

"Exactly. I'm an experienced bricklayer; pay me accordingly."

Seidl played hurt. He wondered whether, under the circumstances, a reference or outstanding wages were in order. But even without Father his business was failing. After Pfeil he had no commissions, only an annex to a shop uptown. Luckily Pfeil persuaded him to pay Father, even though Seidl found him stubborn. Father accepted his final wages, waited a few weeks doing odd jobs until Seidl quietly left town, and focused on his chance. With Seidl seeking his fortunes elsewhere, he applied for work at Heinz Taxenbacher's—as an experienced bricklayer.

The builder soon had him laying cornerstones and throwing fresh stucco over our schoolhouse, on whose second floor I still smelled cheese. Straubling was starting to bustle. There was so much work that old Taxenbacher turned a blind eye when Father worked those small black market jobs. In the meantime Mother did soldiers' laundry and still cleaned at Dr. Deutlinger's, who pulled teeth and rebuilt gums.

Crowns and bridges were part of the upswing in new building. But as I said, there was that one drawback to his practice. Deutlinger's wife had told Mother that even black soldiers sought him out. But when some of them asked to have healthy white teeth gold-capped, an odd custom, the dentist balked. And Mother insisted something was rotten in America.

"And not just its teeth. Hilde Deutlinger wouldn't lie. It's so strange it must have happened."

Again she fought the idea of America, and this gave her ammunition.

"No country," scoffed Father, "has a monopoly on foolishness."

Right then I think he knew it was time to get out of Austria, before things picked up even more and Mother found more ways to object. Even a cuckoo clock might not do. So far even the creek had spared us despite old Krummbacher's dark predictions. Gavrilo's little vendor's shack with its cashier's window had also brought us luck. Fritz Krummbacher accepted that we needed his well, and Berti had eased down from his high horse. Sometimes he even pretended he hadn't seen the dump truck so I could spy it first.

After Father's anger last fall, my biggest challenge was not to go prospecting. We too were becoming builders. Father even got an offer from Ernst Winkler, his foreman at work. Just in time, Mother saw a little article in the *Salzburger Nachrichten*. Our subscription was paying dividends.

She called to Father through our cashier's window as we worked our vegetables. Seconds later she ran toward him by the spring potatoes as he turned soil with his spade. Dark clouds rolled down from the Alps and the snow-capped Weisskönig. Reading the article, Father saw his hopes confirmed. Our future was now.

He could keep his promise to show me Jersey Joe's shores. America had opened possible entry not only to displaced persons, but to former German soldiers with clean pasts. I saw that even Mother had secretly waited for this moment. As usual she'd been contrary, not wanting us to get too comfortable. But her labors and mine, and Father's, had really meant training for America. Now we could be real builders.

Father dropped his spade. "My last shovel of dirt," he announced. "No more turning sacred Austrian soil."

CHAPTER 28

SPRING RUNOFF

Soon after we'd deserted it, the refugee camp was disbanded. Those left were transferred back to Salzburg, to rejoin its dwindling camp and await passage to South America, Canada, or Australia. A few might even stay in Austria or join refugees in Germany. Only we stayed behind in Straubling, for now in our separate hut downstream and holding out for America. The dream now seemed possible.

But it wouldn't happen overnight and this holding action brought surprises. One morning before he went to lay bricks, I heard Father getting ready to work the swollen Salzach River. A fine rain sifted over the cresting flood. Father must have heard it rumble, spotted escaping logs, and thought he'd make one his.

When the snows melted in the spring, some logs slid down from foothill lumber camps into nearby creeks and waterways. Some swirled in the Salzach as spring runoff swept them on. Along the riverbank, like earthen fingers, jetties shored up by rocks periodically reached into the stream. As logs swept close, men waited with long poles tipped with hooks to try to pull them toward shore. It was finders, keepers.

I wanted to join Father as he rummaged for his pole, but he said tersely, "Get ready for school." He glanced at the creek next to our shack, whose waters rhythmically bumped against its little bridge. Poised on the edge of our garden plot over the creek bank, the hulk of the rusting German jeep looked to slide farther down. I paused when Father spoke.

"Scram," he snapped. "Go get your breakfast, *strizi!*"

Already he loped toward the nearest jetty, his heavy pole primed for capture. A pine log swirled within reach—enough firewood for months. Father threw out his pole. Its sharp hook and weight "thunked" on the slippery log. The log began to rotate. As Father fought it, Florian Riedl, our friend the lumberjack, happened by with a load of boards and lumber. He stopped his horse-drawn cart and leaped down the bank to help. With Florian struggling at Father's side, I could watch them without him scolding me. Working the pole, they maneuvered the log closer, careful not to tug abruptly. As it turned in the muddy current, they guided it to shore.

"You'll have firewood for months," said Florian.

"I almost lost it. You've got a nose for wood."

"Glad to help. But I'd better go," said Florian, "my lumber's due uptown. I'll bring my long saw later so we can cut it down. The wood will dry out faster. No one can claim it then, not even old Krummbacher saying we used his jetty."

"First have a drink. Something to warm you up." When Father turned he saw me. "I said get breakfast, rascal."

I protested that I was going. "Just a shot," said Florian. "I've got carpenters waiting. I'll drop Konrad on the way."

They looked at the rising creek as they went inside, and Father grumbled something. Florian nodded. Then Father pulled his schliwowitz from behind the cabbage barrel, little Gavrilo's lingering gift. The fermenting sauerkraut with its tang of rosemary promised heady lunches. I wanted to ask Father for a taste of the brandy, but he didn't look in the mood.

"Hop on!" Florian Riedl said afterward.

I clambered to the hard bench of his cart and we rumbled across the frail bridge across the creek whose churning bumped the struts. Florian studied the water carrying branches and stones from higher up and then glanced up toward the peaks and foothills tethering dark clouds. More rain was due. As he tugged at the horses' reins, the lumber cart drew toward the river's northern bridge.

Florian smacked his lips recalling Father's fragrant schliwowitz. I braced myself for the thumping ride across the bridge above the rushing river. It was gorged with spring runoff and the occasional jostling log, like the one he'd helped Father land. The hard seat rattled my bones. Even above the river's roar, I could hear the fearful noise as Florian's wheels thundered over the bridge.

"About ready?" he shouted.

"What?" I piped up.

"Think they'll let you go?"

We lurched off the bridge back onto gravel road. The fine spring rain kept falling, but Florian's shirt collar was open, and his rakish, green felt hat made his face look wide and square. As his horses champed he guided them. I still wasn't sure what he meant by them letting me go, then realized he meant America.

"It's not for them to say," I told him.

He moved to calm me down, as if he sensed some agitation. "Of course not, Konrad. It's not up to us Austrians. It's up to you and your father, and your mother too."

I could see why Father liked our lumberjack. Florian respected your point of view. In my universe of those you could trust, you could always trust him. Maybe it was his work. In the winters, with the snowy foothills impassible, and using just his body, he'd work loaded sleds down slopes from snowbound lumber camps. It was a time when Palfner's creek bed disappeared in snow, along with the wild raspberries.

Florian could have been killed if anything slipped—the sled on a sharp turn, a runaway log, or even his hobnailed boots. So far he'd survived, or I couldn't have sat right next to him. Maybe the danger was why he never passed up a chance to help us out, like the pine tree he brought our first Christmas along with scraps of lumber, or the fragrant venison he poached on Lechner's mountain range. Just this morning he'd helped Father land that log. They'd both served on the Eastern front.

As we approached a fork in the road, he said he'd better drop me off. "I'm expected at the swimming pool. They need my lumber for cabins."

He meant the changing huts. Hopping down, I said lamely, "I wasn't sure the bridge would hold."

"Oh, it'll hold," he said and laughed. "My father, bless him, carted the logs to build it. Along with planks and struts. Your father, by the way, tells me you like school. You show 'em how it's done!"

On my way uptown to school I couldn't help but linger at Frau Hollinger's bakery window. She must have glimpsed me between customers as I ogled her warm bread, and suddenly she stood in her doorway. I didn't know whether she'd heard about our plans, but she held out a gift. I knew she was a widow, but for the first time I noticed the wedding band on one finger. It looked like an heirloom, worn thin but intricate.

"Go on, Konrad, take it!" she said and smiled. "A little snack for school."

It was one of her crisp, salt-encrusted buns. My knees went weak, and I took my first bite long before I got to school. She always looked so kind that I couldn't hold a grudge against her for hosting Norbert's lunches last summer.

A few shops later I tried to hurry past Luise Gstaltmeier at The Golden Jug as she took delivery of kegs of beer. I'd heard gossip about her and Herr Gruber. Hard to believe, but mostly it was the emperor who surprised me. She looked like she needed attention. She was tall and bony, and her face perpetually sat in judgment.

"Hold on," she said as I dodged past.

I didn't like her tone, but her face broke into that toothy grin.

"Come back Saturday morning."

"Why?" I said, surly.

Last summer's feeding program was past and she'd never matched Frau Hollinger. I planned to pass up the feeding next time if we were still in Straubling, but with the camp gone they'd stop those free lunches too. Even the black bean soup in the camp had shown more imagination than her gruels. Then she said something that made me think she'd heard about our plans. Her grin was gruesome.

"For a special lunch, what else? Wienerschnitzel, potato salad, and a surprise."

My jaw dropped but I managed to accept. Breaded veal cutlet with something extra, what was behind this? My mouth began to water, although I had the sense not to ask, "What's the occasion?"

With all my stops that morning, for the first time I was late for school. The entire class looked up to disapprove. Berti seemed to sneer, and even pretty Monika Waldegger seemed to scold. Only Herbert Mautner refused to react. Throughout the morning Fräulein Seebach asked me pointed questions as if to test my resolve for learning, as on the day I'd tripped Gustl Ponkratz. In review, one question was on the cow's four stomachs, and she looked to me to answer. As the butcher's son, Gustl had answered that question; it seemed so long ago. I nodded toward him, then rattled off the names. Fräulein Seebach seemed disappointed.

But by drawing class that afternoon she couldn't help but like my work. I drew a train rushing past as part of the village scene she'd wanted. Faces blossomed in its windows and a plume of smoke rose from the engine stack. A conductor in dark blue, resembling old Krummbacher, the switchman, stood on the station platform to keep people clear of danger and whistled for the train to start. I deepened the colors with my colored pencils and once more tried to shade and model so flat shapes looked fuller. Fräulein Seebach lingered over my scene but chose not to flatter my technique. Either she was still disappointed I'd been late or she didn't want to spoil me.

"You've got travel in your blood, don't you? It must be exciting," she said.

That again made me wonder about her own travel plans. How well did she know this Curtis Bishop from Texas? Who was this American major with the pencil mustache and odd cropped hair, parted right down the middle, and would we eventually encounter her in America? She looked calm and patient, as if giving it thought.

When the school day finally ended I left with Herbert Mautner. Our book bags bounced on our backs as we walked past the Ponkratz's butcher shop, but we didn't run into Gustl. When more rain slammed down, we ran toward Herbert's house and dodged inside the musty hallway. From indoors it was good to see the rain come down. Finally Herbert went upstairs, and I hurried home.

Even from a distance I could see Florian Riedl's cart stopped before our hut by the swollen creek. The little bridge across it creaked as the water rose. The torrent carried stones and branches that scoured its banks as its waters crept up toward our hut. Teetering on the creek bank above its mouth into the river, the abandoned German jeep looked ready to come down.

CHAPTER 29

A FEARFUL CREAKING

Finally the rusty hulk plopped into the swollen creek. That changed the water's flow and caused the creek bank to hollow out, just before the river and below our garden plot. I watched the torrent work in fascination and forgot to go inside. For now the rain had stopped, but I knew the waters hadn't crested. With last winter's extra snowfall, the rain might release more snow cover. Things didn't look good as rocks and branches scoured the fallen jeep. They filled its broken seats and churned against its rusty doors. Its hull actually seemed to inch toward the river from the water's force.

Just then I forgot Arkansas and its triumph by good men over evil. I recalled old Krummbacher's words about wild water, but I thought Austria needed drama. I also remembered Father's angry words: "They put this camp right on a flood plain."

Only this time we'd chosen to move from the camp and into greater danger. I focused on our shack and Florian's lumber cart before it. He must have spoken with Father that morning, primed to help us out. I imagined the sauerkraut barrel teetering if his cart were needed to trundle it away. The rain picked up again. "Get inside, *strizi!*" I heard Father call. "You don't need to catch your death."

Mother dropped a towel over my head and unceremoniously dried my hair. At my age it was insulting, but Florian Riedl winked. We spent the day in watchful waiting. Although once more the rain stopped, the worst was far from over. It still rained in the foothills. That afternoon the water rose even higher under the little bridge, its creaking fearful.

Father and Mother had gathered our main goods in one corner of our hut—kitchen pots, plates, clothes, bedding, Father's schliwowitz, and finally Mother's pride and joy, the bulging cabbage barrel. If the water rose too high, we could light out quickly. Florian's cart hovered outside, ready to take us to higher ground and his cabin in the foothills. He had brought along a slab of smoked bacon and rye bread, which we devoured. Father poured out his pale brandy and offered me a whiff. As if in harmony, that evening the waters crested and then subsided, but Florian wasn't fooled.

"It bears watching. I have some errands, but I'll come back."

He found us by lamplight a few hours later. Yes, the waters looked to be subsiding. Mother looked gloomily at the cabbage barrel with its stewing juices. It was hard to even think of carting it. It was like disturbing an old friend. Father probably didn't like the idea, either, but the waters outside were rushing.

He looked at Florian. "What do you think?"

"It's too early. Let's take turns watching. Can you put me up for the night?"

Florian had left his cart outside but walked the horses to Lechner's nearby barn. Father gave him my army cot, which they put up in the tiny kitchen. I slept on clothes and blankets, curled up on the floor near Mother and Father. Early during the night the water rose again, and the small bridge creaked to a rhythm. It was like dark music. I didn't sleep from the excitement and Florian's snoring in the kitchen.

From time to time, as they took turns watching the waters, Florian and Father woke me up. Toward morning the worst finally seemed over. By the time we usually had breakfast and I went to school, the frail bridge over the creek swayed only slightly.

"I think that's it," said Florian as Father clapped him on the back. "But I'll stop by, just to see."

We shared a special breakfast, some of Mother's sauerkraut with its tang of rosemary from deep within the cabbage barrel, along with Florian's rye bread and his smoked bacon. I looked at him as I munched. Our portions were fit for a lumberjack. Father gave me the morning off in case we were still in danger, and suddenly I was almost sorry the waters had crested and yet not swept off our shack. I would miss all this excitement and would have to find more books for real adventure.

After breakfast Father and I took a look outside. With everything over, the jeep had found a resting place. It lay far down the creek close to its mouth on the Salzach, its metal carcass half buried by rocks and silt. Some of our tomato patch on the bank above was gone, collapsed into the creek. The Austrians would finally have to drag off the eyesore of a jeep, Father said, and finally end the war.

He thought Kurt Pfeil would be pleased, though he probably drove a jeep in Africa. His driving school would depend on cars that ran. Although Father said little, he was probably very grateful to Florian for standing by with his lumber cart. He would have hated to ask anyone else for help, especially old Krummbacher in his switchman's house just above by the railroad tracks. He had predicted our near catastrophe. Or worse, to hear Spitz and the others snicker at our disaster. Luckily the refugee camp was gone, and we'd had Florian's help.

As always Father found humor in our predicament. "One thing's for sure," he said back inside, "if a flood had ever hit that stinking camp, it would have washed off the stink. And forced the Austrians to do right by us and move us from the flood plain."

"Hans," Mother said, "this isn't the time."

Still, I got to stay away from school that morning and felt special. And if I got any questions, I could proudly tell my tale. But when I finally got back, I didn't feel all that heroic.

Herbert asked, "Where have you been?"

"A threat of flooding," I said nobly, as if that explained everything.

Fräulein Seebach seized on the occasion for a science lesson about the power of nature—the cycle of rain falling, water evaporating, clouds forming, and more rain to nourish crops. "It's majestic and eternal," she said almost wistfully. "But as you know, children, too much rain can fall."

She looked at me to explain. She meant the power of floods.

I glanced at Berti, who'd seen the creek rise from his father's yellow house. But as my teacher and classmates, slightly jealous, looked to me for the wonderful details, I clammed up. An aftertaste of that morning's sauerkraut burped up in my throat. Suddenly I didn't want to talk about our shack or flood plains or even forces of nature. I didn't want to be a lesson plan, even with kindly Fräulein Seebach looking at me and Monika Waldegger sympathetic.

After school Herbert Mautner told me a far more interesting tale.

"They caught up with him in the mountains," Herbert said, "near Lienz and the *Plöckenpass.*"

The pass lay much farther south, on the other side of the Alps toward Italy. Herbert was speaking of the guard at the camp for the Russian prisoners. The haunting story was a tale nobody wanted to talk about, but Herbert gave me pieces. We stood outside the butcher shop, fat sausages coiled in its window. No bovine stomachs.

I saw Gustl Ponkratz scurry inside, helping out behind the counter. It was good to see him do honest work, even if not straightening rusty nails like me. Herbert wasn't interested in going to talk to him. The clouds again promised rain, with patchy sun. Herbert waited as if to add to the suspense.

"What was he up to?" I finally asked.

"The obvious, my father thinks. Skulking south toward Rome, trying to look like a peasant. Mostly moving at night even though it's damned cold up there. Eventual goal, South America."

Working at the district court, Herbert's father saw files, heard gossip, and knew more things than most. I envied Herbert.

"Your father gets all the good stuff," I said.

"Not so much about Otto Jabuka. Most everyone knew him as a bad one. If that patrol hadn't nabbed him, he'd be on his way to Argentina."

"Who's going to get him finally?"

"I suppose whoever wants him most," scoffed Herbert. "Alive or dead. It's all political, says my father. The British got him first; the pass is in the British zone. The higher-ups will decide. Jabuka's a bigger fish than just Ingrid Klein running off with that Serb."

That would have been Zoran Zarić.

"The Russians will want him for guarding those prisoners," Herbert continued, "I take it for propaganda. But they would have killed those comrades anyway, if they'd ever escaped to back home. Seen too much of the West. And they wouldn't keep Otto Jabuka in Vienna if they got him. You can be sure they'd have other plans if he survived interrogation."

Much of Vienna was in the Soviet zone. Anyway, this news had stopped us in our tracks, even though I didn't understand all Herbert told me. He was smarter than most of us, but he also heard things from his father that were complicated. It was a little like hearing Father talk about world politics and Korea. But his news tickled my ears as my eyes caressed Ponkratz's sausages, though I hardly saw them.

"My guess is they'll take him to Salzburg first," Herbert said, "although that doesn't make sense. Unless it's just for transit, until a final decision."

I understood that.

"It takes time to sort these things out. I don't think Austria will want him. The Americans probably want him most, but only to hand him to the Germans. The Germans would try him; they'd want to show awareness."

I wasn't sure why they would want to show awareness but somehow I thought about the dossier on Lechner. "I don't even know what he looks like."

"Jabuka probably went into hiding long before you ever got here. My father thinks he's a Croat, but with a German mother. In his dossier he looks squat and pock-marked. Didn't I show you his picture that time you read about the buried men?"

"No, I would have remembered."

"Then I'll show you another time," said Herbert. "Jabuka even has a brother, a just released American prisoner of war. Probably won't show up around here, either. Anyway, Jabuka's face is all jaws and cheekbones, like building blocks. Sandy-haired below that naked skull. Somehow wound up in the Wehrmacht at Lechner's camp."

The jutting cheekbones sounded familiar, but I could almost hear Lechner wail. "Did you say Lechner's camp? Don't let him hear you say that."

"Just saying, Konrad. We know the Wehrmacht took over his pasture."

CHAPTER 30

THE TRAIN

Suddenly we heard a raucous shout. Poldi Stiegl and Naz Greiner looked like jostling steers. Fortunately they'd left our class months before when a new teacher, Martin Höller, took over the students abandoned by Ingrid Klein. Now they reminded us right before their cousin Gustl's butcher shop.

"If this weren't uptown," sneered Naz, "we wouldn't bother to speak first."

Behind the counter of the butcher shop I saw Gustl glimpse his country cousins but decide to ignore them. The town church faced the market square circled by budding chestnut trees. Across the way stood Meindl's with its aroma of roasted coffee beans. I didn't think Naz wanted to run into his teacher or the meddler Klamm. Their job was to make us good Austrians, even outsiders like me.

Naz looked right to left. As he got close I smelled the same stale odors that steeped his woolen sweater—old cheese, ancient sweat, an undertone of stern soap. His granny must have knitted it using wool scavenged from worn-out sweaters. The gray wool set off the green trim around its wrists and neck. Naz had grown since leaving us; his neck was thick. The leering Poldi joined him.

With my growth spurt still delayed, I felt stronger next to Herbert. "I thought we learned to get along," I said, "as classmates with Inge Seebach."

"Those are bygones, *zugroasta,*" said Naz.

"Get lost," said Herbert, towering over him and Poldi.

Poldi looked me over, but they pulled back. "We wouldn't dirty our hands. Don't think we don't see through the foreigner," he told Herbert. "Once a *zugroasta,* always greasy."

They shuffled off, but the threat hadn't ended. It was just the reminder I needed to make me appreciate America, in case I had doubts. If I played my cards right these last months, I could avoid them entirely. My next encounters would be with Americans. Of course first I'd visit Luise Gstaltmeier for her breaded veal.

"I'm surprised those goons are Gustl's cousins," Herbert said.

"So's Gustl. Have you noticed he avoids them? Even Ingrid Klein didn't deserve them," I said, enraged. "It's probably why she ran off with that Serb. Did you see how big they're getting? I'd like to break their noses." Then I recalled I'd almost done that to Gustl.

"Easy, Konrad. They're just your average shits."

"Damn it, it's the growth spurt. Everyone's getting a head start."

"There's not much you can do, it's inborn," said Herbert, still our class clinician. "But that's also a good sign. My father's big; so's yours. I just got started early."

That calmed me down until I thought of Luise's soups. It would take some pretty special veal to erase that memory. And even with a late growth spurt, I'd never quite catch Herbert.

"But in your case, guess who'll reap the benefit?" Herbert added dryly. "America and Jersey Joe."

That hurt. Father didn't want me boxing, and right now I'd be a flyweight. I shouldn't have told him about my idol.

"I suppose you know the camp's been closed," I said changing the subject. "A recent train took all the inmates, except for my family."

"I meant to ask you about that. You're the only ones left behind, aside from one Royalist. I think a Ratko Radić. Is that how you say it? Unbelievably, I hear he's selling insurance."

Just then I remembered someone else left behind, someone I'd almost forgotten. Herbert must not have known Herr Gruber. But how did he know about our staying? It must have been my being late this morning, or he heard from Berti.

"We took over the Serbs' little vending store," I said. "My father moved it by the river right under Berti's nose."

Herbert didn't mention our heavy rains. "Sooner or later, aren't you going too?"

"We're holding out for America."

"Might as well. What are your chances?"

"Better now, I think." Despite Father's confidence, suddenly I wasn't so sure. I didn't want to jinx our luck. Just in case things didn't work out I still wanted Herbert for my friend. Never get too comfortable, as Father always said.

"Good for you, but bad for us. Austria needs thinkers."

His words made me feel sheepish. Even if I had something to give, I wasn't sure I'd give it to Austria. "I'll write you if we go so we can stay in touch."

"Do that. Anyway, old Krummbacher must hate having you right under his nose."

"He lets us use his well. Berti likes to twist the knife, but we need their water."

"We should find a way to fix him."

I reserved my purest malice for Naz and Poldi. "He's not worth the bother."

"I heard he thumbed his nose when the train passed."

"That was probably to show off. He just wanted to be the first to see it, to call out it was coming. Switchman's due. Maybe he'll grow up once I'm in America. At least old Krummbacher did his duty; he still set the switch." I paused and looked at Herbert. "Want to see something interesting?"

After all our talking, we still stood before the Ponkratz's butcher shop, my eyes still stroking the plump sausages. I glimpsed Gustl hopping behind the counter, still helping out. Anton Ponkratz's lone car stood out front. Until Herbert wanted to fix Berti, I'd almost forgotten about Naz and Poldi.

When we finally left the butcher shop we talked before Frau Hollinger's, dwarfed by her chestnut tree. After all this time I could never get enough of the salt-encrusted pretzels and loaves in her window. Her doorbell chimed as housewives came and went with their shopping nets. Finally we worked our way from uptown to the slope down toward the Salzach River.

Shafts of sunlight cut through the clouds, and the river below meandered like a silver band. It flowed toward Lechner's bottomland where the soldiers maneuvered. Near his barn it turned abruptly toward the northern peaks hiding Salzburg. Closer to us stood the warehouse, our former barracks.

"It's what's left of the camp," I pointed out. "They'll tear it down and save the lumber. Right now it's on Palfner's pasture."

"It stood on his pasture since long before the war," Herbert said. "Palfner must be relieved the refugees are finally gone."

As we walked toward the empty barracks, we saw fresh barbed wire along the road between the river and the pasture. The wire fenced in Palfner's grazing cows. The pied local breed, *Pinzgauer*, plopped their sloppy pies in the grass while grazing on young shoots right by the wire. Palfner could probably see them from his farm in the foothills, if he didn't hear them moo. Or maybe he had Susi Palfner and her little brother watch. We slipped under the barbed wire.

This time Franz didn't stand out front on his crutches to scold me about my chewed-on loaf of bread. Just inside the entrance the usual draft rose from the floor boards. Somewhere I heard the roof leak. Palfner's farmhands had begun to dismantle our pine partitions.

Herbert looked around. "What a shitty way to have lived."

I recalled Stjepan Šlajfer calling it a dump, but also Ludwig and Franz and their chess matches. "It had its moments."

"At least you didn't croak like those Russians."

That much was good. Luckily something diverted me. Most of Franz and Ludwig's walls, with their drawings on brown paper, still stood, including the grimy corner of our final chess match. Outside, as if far away, I heard the treacherous Salzach.

Herbert studied the rendered drawings. "Nice. An almost surgical precision."

I thought he'd understand. "They're exact, but also drawn with feeling. You can almost touch the skin."

Herbert laughed. "Now I know what inspires your art. But what would Fräulein Seebach think?"

"She doesn't need to know. Anyway, she likes my drawing. My father doesn't think drawing matters, but these are much better than mine."

For now Father focused only on America and my education. His dreams didn't include boxing or even art, unless they somehow came with school.

"Has Berti seen these? He'd probably shit himself," said Herbert.

In the light cast by the dusty window panes, the paper cheeks caressed the broken walls. Palfner and his hired hands, in ripping out wood planks for the lumber, had torn off some of the penciled rosary or ripped through plump behinds. I heard water drip over little Jiři's corner in the Kratky's partition, but ours and the Pfeifer clan's were dry and intact.

Very carefully—Herbert loaned me his pocket knife—I peeled off a souvenir, a patch of penciled skin. As I folded it up, I wondered where I'd hide it. I could still hear Mother say, "Disgusting."

Just the same, it was important to me to show these walls to Herbert. I'd miss him. On our way out I looked up toward the railroad tracks beyond the cows and barracks. Herbert hadn't seen the train of refugees leave weeks before, but once again I seemed to see it float past. I'd been hoeing weeds in our vegetable plot and looked up when Berti shouted, "They're coming!"

It had been our turn to feel abandoned. Faces and arms hung from the train windows, and everyone seemed to know our shack. On their way to temporary quarters back in Salzburg, the refugees waved a last goodbye. Mother had left her laundry shed and waved as the train passed. A white shirt and black tie flicked past, Toni Spitz with his wife, Ilon. Others waved madly, knowing exactly where to spot us. A blurred Stipe Baumann skipped past—another one bound for Australia. In the last window I glimpsed Wilma Hutz and her laughing Gerda and Hedwig, with Brazil their fate. As if predicting one of my later drawings, their faces looked like blossoms.

I thought of Klaus Sekyra's mysterious switchman and the bridge washed out by a storm. Before my eyes could capture everyone, the hooting train was gone.

CHAPTER 31

REBORN

So often it was feast or famine, as I came to realize our hectic last days in Austria. Just as our plans for America sped closer, I'd felt an unexpected melancholy seeing our dingy camp with Herbert, and again when the train skipped past. Then Frau Hollinger gave me that fragrant bun, and toothy Luise Gstaltmeier promised a surprise. Austria seemed to clutch at us just as we planned to flee. A final hitch came when Ernst Winkler, Father's foreman, offered to build us a house.

"The firm of Taxenbacher will donate prime land in the foothills—a lot with a splendid view. And the labor and materials. We're all friends here, Hans," he added. "Austria needs you."

"What about the firm of Taxenbacher?"

"It needs your skills," Ernst said, grinning. "One hand washes the other."

"It's a generous offer. A view from above the Salzach, instead of hoping it won't rise," mused Father. "Ernst, I wish I could consider it. I know you had a lot to do with this. But the fact is, for us America's all settled. But stop by before we leave and have a serious drink. I expect Florian Riedl too. We'll have his finest schnapps. Before the Serbs pulled out, I also grabbed some of their schliwowitz!"

That softened the blow for Winkler, more Father's friend than his foreman. It also made me think that now Father was pretty sure about America. But the next day, as he told it, old Heinz Taxenbacher called him into his imposing office overlooking the square before the church.

"What's this I hear, Kemper? Who'd make you a better offer?"

The stocky builder brooked no opposition. His face had the shape of a fierce diamond, formed by hard cheekbones, a sharp chin, and a tuft of gray hair on top.

"Herr Baumeister, you've been very kind. But I'm afraid it's destiny," Father said.

"Nonsense, Kemper. Your future's here, in the new Austria."

Father couldn't help but savor the irony after his first winter in Straubling shoveling snow off railroad tracks. He hadn't even consulted Mother about Winkler's offer, I learned later, and he didn't say what made him so sure about America that he could refuse Taxenbacher. But I was flattered when he told me what he'd told the builder.

"You've treated us very generously, Herr Baumeister, and I trust I've repaid your confidence. But we're decided. My boy and I are destined to discover America."

Heinz Taxenbacher saw that commands were useless and pounded his desk. "*Dann geh'n S' halt nach Amerika!* Then go to your America!"

In fact our dream of America had become relentless and inevitable. Whatever had made Father so sure, his words about destiny could as easily have meant *predestined*. For weeks I'd enjoyed our visits to Salzburg for the preparations and formalities, and we revisited the refugee camp where we'd first met the emperor. Only a minor hitch happened, as if to keep us honest.

As a fine spring rain fell over the Mirabell Gardens, it turned out my birth certificate had been lost or confiscated before we fled from Yugoslavia. It would have happened long before we got to Salzburg, most likely before Mother thought of leaving Grandfather behind. The Communists probably didn't want even one extra German speaker to exist officially.

Father immediately found our hometown friends, the Eberhardts. We saw them regularly in the Salzburg camp, and they'd first written us about Grandfather. In fact on our first trip back to Salzburg Mother insisted on asking about him. We knew he had died soon after we fled Tito's camp, but she needed more. His fate was the one thing that hurt most as we prepared for America.

Old Resi Eberhardt shook her head. "He's in God's hands, Anni."

Mother dabbed her eyes. "What exactly did Lenschi say?"

Lenschi Kleitsch, also from our hometown, had passed through Salzburg to join relatives in America. She had fled our prison camp after us, in the winter after the typhus took Grandfather.

"The typhus was no surprise," Resi said. "No medicines, no soap, and the bedbugs everywhere. I'm sure you knew it better than I could ever imagine."

Old Peter Eberhardt just listened.

"Did Lenschi know? And actually see him?" asked Mother helplessly.

"She always did like to exaggerate, but I'm sure she did. She saw them carry him out, the way they carried out so many." Resi crossed herself. "God rest their souls."

"It's good Lenschi has family in America," conceded Mother, "and not in South America."

She was thinking of Nanschi Massong and the floozy. Only she wasn't quite resigned. Recalling our goodbye to Grandfather—her father—she suddenly began to sob, long groans from deep inside her. Father put his arms around her. It was as if talking about Grandfather's death before hometown folks finally released her sorrow. As she shook, Father's arms only deepened her sobs.

Peter Eberhardt and Father shook their heads. I could tell Father wanted her to have this talk, and he hated what had happened but was resolved to look forward. He turned the talk to America and finally asked the Eberhardts to help make it official that I even existed. I couldn't enter America otherwise.

"Could you?" he said. "We'd be very grateful."

Resi and Peter happily agreed to sign a notarized statement about my birth in our obscure German-speaking farm town half an hour north of Belgrade. For some reason Father got my birth date wrong, so officially I was born one day later, on St. Joseph's Day. That was fine with me, since Grandfather's name was Josef. The error would make no difference, anyhow, in whether I'd enjoy Luise's wienerschnitzel or when I'd start my growth spurt. By the time Mother noticed, the mistake was done and documented. I'd be entering America with pretensions.

The Eberhardts grinned shyly as the camp's spiritual adviser, *campi curi* Matthias Steinwasser, countersigned with a flourish. I was reborn even before we reached America—as the newborn Konrad Kemper.

Father clapped my back so hard I coughed. "Now you exist officially. And while you still have time, eat your fill of Austrian bread. In a few more weeks American bread will have to do."

That didn't sound good. I thought about Frau Hollinger's fragrant loaves.

Mother protested. "Hans, people are watching."

But it was just the grinning Eberhardts and the puzzled curate.

I stood sheepishly before them as the freshly minted Konrad Kemper, my hand extended as if to hail Jersey Joe.

But my rebirth wasn't all that was new. I still spied cigarette stubs in the Mirabell Gardens, as I'd once done for the emperor. But at the Hotel Europa workers cleared rubble from its dank lower stories and bombed-out basement, where I'd once seen rats. The Rainerstrasse and nearby streets had begun to bustle as shop windows filled with more goods. Along the Elisabeth Quay the Salzach River flowed sedately and majestically, unlike its wilder twin upstream at Straubling, where it carried Ponkratz's cattle tripe and scooped up little Jiři. One night we even stayed in their barracks with the Eberhardts before we returned to Straubling. I couldn't sleep from the excitement and because old Peter snored.

CHAPTER 32

A PRIZE COLT

Suddenly our plans for America couldn't have gone any better. Things went smoothly and relentlessly, as if Austria couldn't wait to spit us out. Despite everything we passed our physicals, although the émigré doctor in Salzburg found me thin.

"He'll fill out; he's a Kemper," Father said. "Add American food, the light. He'll be big like me and strong as a horse." He patted me down as if checking a prize colt.

The doctor grunted. He tapped my chest and back and lowered his stethoscope to my naked skin. I winced at the cold metal. Father winked.

"You will please breathe deeply," the doctor rumbled in his Russian accent. "Indeed. A growing boy, the lungs don't quite keep up."

His words electrified me. It suddenly dawned on me why Father's shoulders seemed a little unfamiliar; they were at the level of my eyes. Was I being reborn in more ways than one? Having waited so long for the growth spurt, I'd begun to lose faith. But Father seemed to lack all appreciation for my torments.

"It's the family history," he said lightly, "another reason he'll fill out." Out of nowhere, he told the doctor, "But I'll be damned if he'll box."

"In that case, absolutely," said the Russian doctor, as if used to appraising both livestock and athletes. "He has the making of a winner. In America, indeed, combined with the food and light. But for sure, we need a specimen."

He wanted a vial of my amber piss.

It felt appropriate after Father's teasing. I wished for a potted plant to water but reconsidered. Behind a white curtain, I clenched my fists and gave. It helped that it rained outside. Finally my checkup was done. Mother and Father had already passed their physicals, despite the black bean soup. The rain outside seemed never-ending, but I floated from the doctor's office, feeling good and gangly.

We tramped down the corridor toward another appointment, a meeting on destinations in America and possible American sponsors. Meanwhile the rain fell over Salzburg's roofs and cobbled streets, over Mozart's ghostly birthplace tucked into a square, and over the iron railroad bridge swaying in the Salzach River. As it gurgled down drainpipes and gutters, I seized the opportunity.

"It's starting," I said.

"What's that?" Father said absently.

"The growth spurt," I said ominously.

"It's too early."

"I feel taller. Didn't the doctor agree?"

Father looked a little skeptical, and it took me a while to explain that I was seeing his shoulders at the level of my eyes. He looked me up and down.

"It'll happen when it happens. You can be sure it won't be pretty."

That hurt. "What do you mean?"

"At first your nose and ears will stick out, along with your hands and feet. You may trip and stumble. Even your voice will change. That's when you'll finally know."

That didn't sound good, except for the voice. I must have looked pleading. But he finally reassured me he'd gone through just those same stages.

"Enough now; just relax."

The rest of that day paled in comparison—even our meeting on American sponsors. I persevered from habit more than anything, and kept my ears open and my mouth shut. First we went down the stately corridor of the old Hapsburg building that overlooked the majestic river. Although it needed paint, the building had survived the bombing. Had the Americans spared it because they'd planned to use it?

Still, it was odd that in all our processing we hadn't yet seen real Americans. Even the review of sponsors would probably be with another Austrian, some toady who spoke German but worked for the Americans. Maybe they were just too busy. I glanced out the towering windows. Across the river at the little bridge, the *Mozartsteg*, I glimpsed the narrow passage toward the Mozart square. Father thought that one day, just maybe, Salzburg might again become a goal for music lovers, even American pilgrims.

Suddenly, coming toward us in the corridor, we saw none other than Norbert Pfeifer and his jabbering granny. We hadn't yet reached our appointment and couldn't duck into another office. Granny Pfeifer sidled greedily, like a crab. I thought Norbert had long ago left for Canada to finally take up hockey, but here he was, green-eyed and lantern-jawed. To my surprise, it wasn't bad to see him.

On Mother's face I saw no eagerness. Right now Granny Pfeifer was probably the last person she wanted to see. Norbert said "hullo" as his granny moved her mouth. Looking at him, I saw the top of his red hair from a little higher up. I hadn't seen him for a while and noticed. It gave me strength.

"How are things?" I said, superior.

Before he could speak his granny sniffed, "Surprised to see us, aren't you? Wouldn't you know we've been delayed? I thought I'd show Norbert how the Americans live."

What Americans? We hadn't seen any, unless Father wasn't telling. So far we'd seen Austrians and that Russian doctor. The rain continued sifting down. It fell like a mist over the copper cathedral dome, the bridges over the river, and the shrouded fortress on the hill. It was Salzburg's rite of spring, its infamous *schnürelregen*.

"And you," wheezed Granny Pfeifer, "so finally it's your turn?"

"Still off to Canada?" Father said tersely.

"Of course, of course, it's good enough for us," said Granny, as if to rebuke us for America. "Then it's all settled? You haven't run into problems?" she said hopefully.

Her hazel eyes had narrowed. I'd actually never seen her this close up, despite having her as our camp neighbor and hearing the Pfeifers' breakfast noises. Her face was square like Norbert's, with pale brown spots that might once have been freckles. Her teeth looked strong enough to bite off Norbert's head, if ever he dared to ask her for another spoon. She would probably do the same when he wanted his first hockey stick, out in Medicine Hat or Moose Jaw.

"But now we're all set," she pattered on. "Norbert's uncle can't wait to see us."

I thought I could have. Mother asked about her granddaughter, Kati.

"Fit, very fit. She takes after me," said Granny Pfeifer. "I left her at Graumichl's, our friends here in camp." Now she turned to me, as if to get some digs in. "And how is school?"

"Fine," I said tersely.

"And your grades?" she inquired. "Still think you're the best?"

She probably had that from Norbert, although I didn't recall bragging. I looked from her moving mouth to Norbert, his eyes green like tarnished groschen.

"They're better than Norbert's," I said about my grades.

"*Eigenlob stinkt!*" she got in her zinger. It was a standard phrase parents used whenever their young got uppity. "Self-praise stinks."

"Not in his case," Father said firmly, surprising me. He took Mother's arm. "Anni, time for our appointment."

"It was good to see you both," Mother said with finality. "Have a safe trip to Canada."

"To be sure," said Granny Pfeifer.

"Moose Jaw," chimed in Norbert.

The word *lantern-jawed* fit him perfectly.

"I think you'll like ice hockey, Norbert," I told him. "Even Sepp Bradl would if he ever had the chance. You'll probably make a fine goalie." I actually meant it. He'd be in harm's way as a goalie, but from what I had heard about the sport, his chunky build and iron jaw would let him punish others. "The ice and snow will do you good. Just play hard and you'll keep warm."

Norbert's tight face grew easy. They finally waved goodbye, and we returned to America. Our great interview about American destinations turned out to be preliminary, and Mother and Father kept me quiet. After they completed more forms, Father said we were being carefully screened.

Colombia, Canada, or Australia took almost anyone, but for America you needed real visas.

When we finally got to decide where to go, it was odd to see a pale Austrian sitting at his desk. He worked for the Americans but looked like a clerk. Despite the tall windows behind him from the days of the Austrian empire, with a majestic view of Salzburg and the misty fortress on the Mönchsberg, l felt cheated. I realized I'd wanted to deal with at least one American, maybe even a consul. The dusty Austrian bowed slightly, motioning for us to sit.

He laid aside his cigarette, careful to snuff it out so as not to waste precious tobacco. Even so, smoke still curled through the stuffy office, and a tickling crept up my throat. I was able to stop from coughing, but the faint Camel trademark on the stubbed-out cigarette reminded me of Herr Gruber and the stubs I'd once found for him. Behind the Austrian's desk, in the gray light from his stately windows, an American flag held spangled stars.

Now the clerk opened our folder to talk of work and sponsors. "I'm afraid Milwaukee's fallen through," he said. "Another family's going there."

That left us two main choices. We could go to New Jersey or Chicago, due to sponsors just then available. A truck farmer in the Garden State offered housing and contract labor, and a Catholic parish in Chicago could also sponsor us. Father acted as if rolling dice, yet chose quickly.

Without looking at Mother, he said, "Chicago."

But they must have talked before, or he would never live it down. In fact, whoever had raised Jersey Joe, I was sure she resembled Mother. Father glanced from the clerk toward her but sounded as if he spoke to me. That flattered me. Whatever went through his mind, he seemed to think Chicago was our better choice. I was sure my future figured in. And Chicago had no Jersey Joe. The Austrian looked satisfied. He glanced at his extinguished cigarette and penciled something into our file.

I'd expected more from this meeting, except Father seemed so sure. "We're builders, you and I," he told me afterward. For once he didn't mention boxing. And found Chicago right for me.

But it wasn't until two weeks later that everything felt just right. One of the soldiers for whom Mother laundered stopped by with dirty wash.

I knew him but not from close up. In his floppy olive-green fatigues the blond American looked burly yet easy and good-natured. As he doffed his cap, his duffel bag sat on his bulging shoulders and his cropped hair bristled like a boy's. Even though he lacked a handlebar mustache, I saw how much he looked like Field Marshall Paul von Hindenburg, the German hero of Tannenberg and World War I. I recalled an old photo of him that Father once showed me in a book.

The bear-like soldier didn't know it, but he looked like a cousin of the heroic Hindenburg. I almost wanted to tell him, but I didn't know English, and he stumbled over his German. Besides, I wasn't sure he'd want to look like a German hero—even the mythic Hindenburg.

It looked like more rain, and the American was about to trudge back to his garrison. After all her resisting Father about America, now Mother couldn't control her excitement. Somehow she made the soldier understand we'd go to America. The American set down his bag, and his face broke into a crooked grin.

"Welcome to America," he said.

Just then, almost by accident, America finally came true for me. The American had said what I'd hoped to hear in Salzburg. There remained just the formality of the ocean crossing. The soldier repeated in broken German:

"*Willkommen zu Amerika.*"

CHAPTER 33

THE EMPEROR'S CLOTHES

Soon after, Father put the finishing touches on the wooden trunk he'd built. He had carefully sawed and tapped in the nails, then painted it green—the only color he happened to have. Once it was dry, as I watched, he stenciled on it the name and address of a Catholic relief organization in New York that would take delivery for us. Like many German speakers he mixed up final *v*'s and *w*'s and stenciled "Nev York." He seemed to want a perfect trunk, so I didn't want to tell him. The address looked good anyway—exotic and faraway. I would have liked to help him paint the letters, but it was time for me to go. Father looked too absorbed to say much.

"Do your duty, *strizi,*" he seemed to snort as he brushed. I said goodbye and walked uptown to Luise Gstaltmeier's to claim my breaded veal.

At her oak entrance I gave the door chime a good ring. She looked dour when she opened. The Golden Jug again was quiet; it was too early for real customers. I took my old seat below the stag's head, still half wary it might drool. It didn't, and her wienerschnitzel was magnificent. Now I was the one to drool.

"*Lass dir's schmecken,*" Luise said as before. "Enjoy your meal." This time she seemed to mean it.

The veal's breaded crust was golden and the meat white and moist within, nudged by butter lettuce and spring potatoes flecked with parsley. Just one thing was missing—Frau Hollinger's fragrant buns. Now Luise brought those in too, fresh from her bakery. She didn't say much, as if it hurt to smile, but even plopped down a soda bottle.

I managed a hoarse "Thank you."

Biting down, I watched her bony figure retreat to the kitchen. When she opened its door, I glimpsed someone's trouser legs at a chair by her counter. The door hid the body, but the pants looked familiar. Piping of forest green ran down the outside of the legs. It couldn't be, I thought but mulled it over, savoring each bite of veal. Still, I couldn't help imagining Norbert, feasting on veal and vanilla last summer at kindly Frau Hollinger's. Each bite of the tender veal was like a summons. I closed my eyes.

After I finished Luise brought in dessert, an airy *kaiserschmarren*. The "emperor's omelet" was the result of an egg-rich batter, scrambled in a hot pan. She served this concoction with apple compote and dusted with confectioner's sugar.

My Austrian journey was complete.

"Now you know the real Austria," she seemed to rebuke me.

I resolved never again to speak ill of Austria or even Norbert.

My mouth was full as she opened the door back into the kitchen; this time I watched carefully. The gray trouser legs were gone. I wondered how to tell Father so he'd believe me. When I said goodbye, I thanked Luise stiffly. She wished me good fortune in America. Outside bloomed the chestnut trees, the candelabra of their blooms shedding a white, magical dust. In a few days Father and I were to visit the humorless Monsignor Bruck. For now my gut caressed its cargo. I turned and waved back at Luise. For a minute I thought I'd miss her.

I walked on, reborn. It wasn't just Father's error in my birth date or the growth spurt. On the way back to help him with the trunk, if he wanted help, I glimpsed Herr Gruber. The emperor was whistling. I'd never heard him whistle. He didn't see me and walked on with a purpose, maybe on his way back to his inn, Zum Hirschen. As always he wore his fraying Austrian costume, the traditional gray wool with forest green cuffs and lapels, and that green stripe down each trouser leg. In my mind a name clicked in place—kaiserschmarren, the emperor's omelet.

As I entered our shack, I saw that Father had finished stenciling the wooden trunk with the address in "Nev York." He had used some of Florian's choicest lumber to build it—fragrant pine—and now admired his work.

"How was it?" he said dryly.

"Unbelievable," I said, suddenly breathless at the memory.

"That good or that bad?"

"It was wonderful. Mother would have been amazed."

"What did you have?"

I didn't stint on the details.

"What's behind this bounty?"

"Don't know. Maybe she wanted to make up for all that soup she fed me last summer."

Father laughed, but I thought I knew what had happened.

It was too much of a coincidence that the emperor had hovered nearby. The name "kaiserschmarren" had tipped me off, although Herr Gruber couldn't have known the coincidence. He didn't know he was our emperor. I had heard rumors about something between him and dour Luise. The emperor could have prevailed upon her better nature. Or just maybe, unbelievably, he had actually paid for my feast—as a farewell for me, but costing an arm and leg. How could he afford it? I suddenly didn't want to burden Father with his generosity; he would have tried to repay it. It felt better as a secret between me and the emperor.

As I sat on our empty cabbage barrel, I watched Father perfect his trunk. He gazed at the full address of the Catholic relief organization, a congress of "welfare" or other in New York. It would take not only delivery of the trunk if it got lost but sponsor our Atlantic passage. Father's pine locker matched Mother's cabbage barrel as a labor of love. As he added final touches to the stenciled lettering, he again noted his last meeting with his boss, Heinz Taxenbacher. For some reason he looked at me sternly.

"We're emigrating. But not into internal exile, like Baumeister Seidl. We're getting the hell out, period. No more scooping mortar or shoveling snow off railroad tracks; I don't care if the trains are late."

His sudden anger made his brush slip, but he wiped off the damage. Once again he hammered at his favorite theme, as though hell-bent on my future. "I'm sure your Jersey's Joe's waiting, but not in Chicago. You and I are builders; I'll be damned if you'll box!"

That left art and chess. With my stomach full, I could handle that. And already chess was somehow receding after my lucky coup against Franz. I didn't tell Father about the chess or art, so he could focus on the boxing. I never really thought of boxing even with Jersey Joe my hero. After my talks with Herbert and everything else, it was beginning to dawn on me that art would be my passion. If so, I also knew at some point I'd have to tell him. Art didn't go with Father's dreams of America, whether in New Jersey or Chicago.

In our last days in Austria, I already imagined scenes that needed drawing. I imagined Franz and the artist, Ludwig, on that train with Spitz and Baumann, as their train had floated past me just above old Krummbacher's grassy embankment. Then came little Jiři, scooped up by the Salzach. Mercifully I saw little Gerda skip past on the train with Hedwig, along with Wilma Hutz and the rest, bound for Brazil and other outposts. No matter where I turned, the world brimmed with haunting mystery.

Before me Father lovingly touched up his letters, as if the trunk brought out his own artistic side. His arts were more practical. Through our window, as he finished, the snowy peaks of the Weisskönig shone above our shack like clean jewels. If I'd been on that fleeting train as its wheels spun, its granite peaks would have trembled.

When Herr Gruber stopped by a few days later, we had expected him. Mother came in from our tiny kitchen, and I helped her set the table. After his awkward goodbye at our earlier partition, she felt at home with the emperor. He was an old friend now, although today he seemed forlorn. We had just enough chairs for the four of us.

"It's an honor," he said, courtly. "My great honor to be invited."

He was about to pat my hair but instead tapped my shoulder.

"Yes, young man, it's your time now. Time to embrace opportunity."

The emperor, I recognized, came from another world. We hadn't seen him much during our last months in Austria. It made his arranging for my feast at Luise's all the more daring. A last meal, so to speak, for someone condemned to discover. From Father I had heard the emperor seemed content at his inn, Zum Hirschen, with his pipe and beer at his regular table and just a narrow stairway from his room above. It was a room Dubravka Boban had once cleaned.

The inn's simple rooms were small, Mother knew from Dubravka. He had stopped odd jobs like splitting kindling and got by on his small pension. That was quickly spent on beer, and then he would wait anxiously through the dry spell until his next allotment. But in his letters to his daughter, Erna, he would write he was well, all things considered. "I still have my pride," he would tell Father.

He had begun to realize that we, too, would soon be leaving. By now Mother seemed more eager than Father. Father did what was needed but saw we faced a hard departure. Discipline, he said, would be lacking in America—his "discipline with humanity." I didn't think that was the only reason, but he wanted to visit Monsignor Andreas Bruck for the moral counsel. Father had seen the emperor founder but always saw him with ironic humor. Of course, he would only tell Mother.

"Herr Gruber's spirits derive, so to speak, from living right above the tap."

"Don't make a joke of it, Hans," she would scold.

Mother was always a touch contrary, as if to brake what she saw as some of Father's impulsiveness. But she could also be generous. Only days before we left Austria she had sent me to invite Herr Gruber. After my feast at Luise's, I was especially happy to do it. Mother had even baked a special cake—a *linzertorte*—on the metal stove Father had cobbled together, and which we'd uprooted from our earlier barracks.

The torte was baked after a nostalgic recipe from the days of empire; I don't know how she even managed to get all the ingredients. The name was fitting if cruel. She had forgotten that Herr Gruber's daughter now lived in Linz, right above a bakery. After her savory chicken goulash, we talked over slices of her linzertorte and soon veered toward melancholy.

Luckily Father had brought some beer from uptown, which revived the emperor's spirits. White suds flecked his mustache. As he raised his glass, dark dirt showed under his fingernails, like the dark borders of funeral notices. He praised Mother's goulash. Suddenly she consented to a beer, and that broke the ice. Bravado took hold of our little group, and our pretense at a good time turned into rising spirits. Father even poured me my first gulp of beer. It tingled, slightly bitter, as it scooted down my throat.

We were saying goodbye to the emperor and to Austria, although Austria hadn't really wanted us until now, with one foot out the door. It was as if, no matter how time is spent, its passage was cause for regrets. And somehow Europe had once been home.

Mother even got tipsy. She smiled as Father and Herr Gruber told ancient army stories. When they got racy, she grinned. I'd never seen her like this; I wasn't sure I would again. But finally it was time to say goodbye. The emperor asked whether we would write him.

"Of course," Father said, and Mother added, "We'll hold you in fond remembrance."

Father raised his glass. "Herr Gruber, you'll always be our symbol of the true Austria, the generous old Austria-Hungary that still exists in the hearts of a few."

His sentiments brought tears to the emperor's eyes. "Dear friends," he began, but couldn't finish. When they shook hands, Herr Gruber raised Mother's hand to his lips in the bygone fashion of empire.

"*Küss die Hand, gnädige Frau.* My lady, I kiss your hand."

After all this time I also got to shake the emperor's hand. He suddenly looked shy. "Yes, young man," he said, "now it's on to America! Someday, yes, you'll be someone important. You have the makings, and in America you'll find opportunity."

He stepped out through our cramped door, though not as tall as Stjepan Šlajfer, and felt his way into the night. With the crickets chirping, I recalled the floozy locked in American arms. Intent on walking straight, Herr Gruber's figure diminished on the road back to his inn. Father and Mother watched him for a long time, miserable, and finally went back inside. As if duty-bound, I watched the emperor fade into the summer night.

CHAPTER 34

SNAPSHOTS

It was almost a relief when more visitors stopped by the next day to say goodbye. Father and I looked for more glasses. "If we're short," he finally said, "we'll just drink from the bottle. We're not so prim and proper."

He had one last clear bottle of schliwowitz, again courtesy of little Gavrilo, who'd sold us our hut, and beyond that schnapps from Florian. Of course, Gavrilo would have used the Serbian word. Close to our departure, our vegetable plot outside rested. True to his word, Father had stopped turning Austrian soil. What still grew we ate—cabbages, beans, and tomatoes.

Florian Riedl came by first, followed by the hang-dog driver, Hias. We knew who had arrived as soon as we heard the chattering gravel truck with a missing hood flap. Still in purgatory about the Leghorn he'd run over, the driver hardly dared to look at Mother. Father poured from his last schliwowitz. They raised their glasses.

"Horuck," said Father. "Bottoms up!"

Florian smacked his lips and toasted, *"Prost."*

Still standing, Father refilled the glasses as Mother watched in wonder.

"To America," Florian said.

"To Austria," added Father. I didn't think he meant it but our friend Florian deserved the courtesy. "Anyway, I've stopped gardening. You two help yourselves to fresh vegetables. Better do it soon, though. Krummbacher's sure to reap what's left."

I looked out the vendor's window toward the ripening string beans, tomatoes, and all the other greens I'd tended so lovingly. The plants were almost like younger siblings, having needed my constant care. Franz and Ludwig might have disdained them, but not any soup or goulash with them in it.

Florian glanced at the driver. "We'll be sure to do that, Hans. After we take you up to Salzburg."

"Better do it before," said Father. "But sit down; sit down already."

Florian found a chair by our table, the one Herr Gruber had vacated the day before. Hias settled on the barrel of sauerkraut. I could almost hear a last wad of kraut fermenting deep inside with gassy burps, but the barrel was almost empty now. The round board weighted by a stone was still wedged inside its mouth to hold the pressure on the fermentation. A larger board across the top made the barrel into an extra table, and right now a seat for Hias.

Father offered the driver his last shot of schliwowitz. Mother brought out the remaining linzertorte from our goodbye with the emperor. Lately we were eating well, and I wished for more goodbyes. Neither Florian Riedl nor Father took any torte, but the grateful driver accepted a slice from Mother. She looked conciliatory.

But as we said goodbye to our stream of visitors, the farewells turned to other news. I found the dark rumors fascinating, like Herbert Mautner's buried soldiers.

"Did you hear?" Florian said uncomfortably. "They've nabbed Otto Jabuka."

Of course I knew from Herbert, but I hadn't told Father. Jabuka was a dirty secret, not so different in a way from my once tripping Gustl.

"That should make Lechner happy," Father said.

It didn't. Only minutes later, stopping by with Fritz Krummbacher, Lechner spat his words. "So they finally caught up with that scum. And for what? It won't restore my good name. My pasture will be forever linked to what he did."

"Alois, have a drink," said Father, pouring for the new arrivals. Chunky Lechner's head jerked up at Father's chummy tone.

Old Krummbacher wore his festive dark blue uniform with a railroad man's red trim. Our cramped hut barely held us all, yet it wasn't as near to bursting as the day the Serbian Royalists held their farewell. That was the day Gavrilo Stepić had managed to squeeze an arm through his little vendor's window, to toss out a fistful of bronze change to us boys seething outside.

Father's last schliwowitz was gone. With a nod toward Florian, he said, "Gents, let's try Florian's finest."

"Aha," carped Lechner, suspecting an illegal still.

Once again Father raised his glass. "To Austria."

"And to America!" they retorted, generous.

"To opportunity and the future!" Father added.

"Who the hell was he anyway?" Lechner muttered, focused elsewhere. His cropped mustache lingered above his glass. "Where'd this Jabuka come from?"

"Does it matter?" Florian said. "Probably Germany. Detailed here with his unit."

"Croatia, for sure. With a name like that," said old Fritz Krummbacher.

No one said "Austria."

"Who's this now?" a voice said at the door.

It was Kurt Pfeil, joining us from his next-door construction site. His foundations were up, thanks to Father and France Pregelj, and more stacks of their concrete blocks stood ready to be used to build. In fact his raw main building was up, for now looking like those ruins in Salzburg. Before Seidl disappeared he had finished the basic structure for the carpenters, electricians, and roofers. Taxenbacher's competition had finally buried him. In an Austria that began rebuilding, Seidl sought his fortunes elsewhere. But not before he'd done his share for Pfeil's dreams for the future.

"Otto Jabuka," hissed Lechner, "and those Nazi swine who took my land."

Pfeil stood stiffly, like a stork pondering a frog. He took the shot glass Father offered. "Jabuka, you say? He was just a cog like so many."

He glanced pointedly at Lechner, then at Krummbacher. "Like some who set the switches, and those who coughed up land. Jabuka probably followed orders just like them. Didn't they finally catch up with him, wasn't it up near Lienz?"

Lechner blanched. "Is that what you call it—orders?"

"What were his choices?"

By now everyone was fidgeting.

"Of course he had choices," Lechner huffed. "He not only chose to follow orders, but he did it religiously. He abandoned all restraint, and he did it on my land."

I thought I understood what he meant but maybe not entirely. I'd have to ask Father later. Lechner talked as if someone had made a mess that wasn't authorized.

"Look here, I brought a photo," Lechner added, as if that would explain things. "It's from a party at Stubaier's; he's in it accidentally."

"Ah," said Pfeil, sounding impatient.

Less intent on the future, Lechner pulled out a black and white creased snapshot with serrated borders. It showed the local choir celebrating an anniversary in Ludwig Stubaier's *biergarten*. No one seemed surprised he had it. The folksy *gesangverein* included a beaming Ludwig; Lechner's wife, Konstanze; and even the bony Luise Gstaltmeier. I didn't know she sang.

Off to one side a table stood under a lilac bush, with the guests seated around it glancing toward the camera. One of them had a squat, pockmarked face with jutting cheekbones below a naked skull. He squinted at the camera but was pretty much the man described to me by Herbert. Otto Jabuka, a guard at the POW camp, either hadn't seen the camera or was probably unhappy to have been caught in the snapshot. It was the last anyone had seen of him.

I squirmed between Lechner and Kurt Pfeil to see him from close up and started. Jabuka was heavier, but he resembled the bony stranger at the American dump ground off the riverbank, the unshaven former soldier who had traded me a chocolate bar for stubs of cigarettes. Somewhere near Straubling, Herbert had told me, Jabuka had an older brother.

Father saw me and looked stern. "*Strizi*, go help your mother."

I left reluctantly and didn't find her in our tiny kitchen. Instead she stood outside by our vegetables, as if saying goodbye. Or maybe she'd gotten bored with all the men's talk. As the Salzach River rushed past, the elderberry bush behind her stood in white flower. She didn't look like she needed anything, and I sneaked gratefully back inside. Amazingly no one had touched her linzertorte, except the driver when she had offered. I nudged the tray off to one side in case anyone got ideas. Florian Riedl was asking Hias to drive uptown to get more beer. Father stuffed some bills into the driver's pocket. The truck coughed and chattered off.

Now Pfeil raised his glass. "Well, gentlemen, to the future and fortune. To all the futures we deserve."

He turned toward Father.

"All success in America. Just remember, back here in Straubling the roads will soon fill up with cars. The future won't happen just in America. And I'll be here, teaching everyone to drive toward it. No small thanks to you."

He downed his brandy and gazed out toward his building site.

"France Pregelj sends his greetings," Father said. "Too bad he'll miss your fleet of cars. He would have made a fine mechanic."

Pfeil laughed. "I told you, you refugees are hungrier."

Lechner and old Krummbacher seemed relieved when Pfeil finally left and the subject of Jabuka was laid to rest. Had his camp provided Lechner with Russian labor? Who had switched the prisoners' train toward it? I'd have to check with Father.

As if in answer, Krummbacher muttered to Father, "Even with cars we'll need trains. Aren't you taking a train up north? Well, best be going. More switches to set."

Just before leaving with him, Lechner stared at Florian, the schnapps rising to his cheeks. "One of these days we'll have something to discuss." His eyes looked fixed, but then he shook Father's hand. "It's been a pleasure," he said, surprisingly. "But don't think you'll ever escape Austria."

Father promised to remember it. I knew I would.

Now Hias, the driver, returned with more beer and passengers. Along the road he had picked up Ernst Winkler and Sepp Mittermeier, Father's comrades from work. Winkler clapped Father's shoulder, who began to pour. But Ernst drank his frothing beer straight from the bottle as Mittermeier slugged down a schnapps. Sepp chased it with a beer, then downed another schnapps. The silent driver seemed to mourn all Leghorns.

Back from our vegetable plot, as always practical, Mother brought in a plate of sliced rye bread from a loaf I'd brought from Frau Hollinger's. "You'd better eat something," she told everyone.

"To line your stomachs," said Father.

"Sure you won't change your mind?" teased Ernst Winkler, referring to Heinz Taxenbacher's offer.

"You mean that house up in the hills?" Father asked. "Overlooking the river and valley? I'll admit it's tempting."

"It's not too late to undo things, Kemper."

"I'm sorry, Ernst, it is," said Father.

Sepp Mittermeier drew him aside. "It's a good offer, but you know what? Go where you need to be."

Father looked touched. "You know I trust you, Sepp. You taught me the trade."

Mittermeier put a finger to his mouth. "Don't tell Ernst. But I know opportunity when I see it. Didn't we both desert Georg Seidl?"

Father suddenly looked tired. The goodbyes were wearing on him, and maybe on Mother, and we lacked places to sit. Hias again reigned from the barrel. When Ernst Winkler finally left with Mittermeier, their faces somber, Florian and Hias soon followed in the gravel truck. Our cramped hut felt silent. But first they agreed with Father on the exact hour to drive us to Salzburg. And swore on their honor to pluck our last vegetables.

CHAPTER 35

COWBOYS AND INDIANS

That July I didn't just read about the knockout, I actually got to see it. Father gave me the coins for a cheap front row seat to see *The Jungle Book*. It was his last gift to me in Austria, and it turned out to be like being ringside. Mowgli's story was all right but it couldn't match the pounding newsreel just before it. In the seventh round in Pittsburgh in the state of Pennsylvania, as I craned my neck, Jersey Joe Walcott hammered his rival Ezzard Charles.

It was an awesome feat for a man of thirty-seven, said the announcer, and showed endurance and tenacity—just what Father thought was needed in a son of immigrants. And doubly so, since Jersey Joe had lost before to both Joe Louis and even to Charles.

It was just as amazing to think there was now a way of watching such a fight directly, all of it, from many kilometers away, without actually being there, to see and hear everything, just as it all happened—the roped ring, the glistening sweat, the fighters' biceps, the crunch and snap of gloves. Someday we'd have "television." The idea of distance vision seemed to foretell America and to confirm everything of which I dreamed.

My thoughts got so feverish I already saw us in Chicago after touching down on Jersey Joe's shores. The knockout refreshed me for our final journey—our coming Atlantic voyage and the train ride west from New York to Chicago. I just about forgot Herr Gruber until, almost as an afterthought, Father mentioned his middle name: Amadeus. A heritage from his cultured mother, he said, whose special love was Mozart even though she'd married a farmer back in Bohemia. The arch name seemed just right—a tribute with a hint of melancholy. It even made me think ahead to windswept Chicago in the heart of America. I could already imagine the letter we'd get from the emperor, written in his florid script.

"Yes, dear friends," he would say, "sometimes I walk past what used to be our communal barracks. All that's left of your partition is the rusty nail in the window frame where Frau Kemper would hang her kitchen rag. No one's bothered to remove it. I hear Palfner wants to raze the barracks for the lumber and clear more pasture for his herd, but for now the mayor wants it for a storage shed. A warehouse remains a warehouse. I'm glad you aren't here to see its fate. Your little hut, the other barracks, has been dismantled. The widow's decided not to move in. Forgive me; I'm becoming sentimental."

My imagination got ahead of me, but I could predict most of what he would say from who he was and my last camp visit with Herbert, except for that nail I'd missed.

"My dear friends," the emperor closed, "from your old world, greetings and warmest wishes on the American venture. Your devoted friend, Franz Gruber."

But soon our remaining days in Austria, with Jersey Joe and everything, sped by so quickly I lost track of the emperor. One of our last school days that June, our class went on an outing. I acted bored, but the day off from school had me excited although I tried to hide it. The price of admission for the outing, at least for Gustl Ponkratz, was to steal some lipstick from his mother. Berti Krummbacher saw to that.

Few women could afford lipstick or wore it, but Gustl's father ran the butcher shop. Along with being mayor he also drove that Volkswagen. I had no idea that eventually he might want to transform our old barracks back into a warehouse and city storage shed. Right off Berti began applying Indian war paint to Gustl's face with the stolen lipstick. He worked with a purpose out of Fräulein Seebach's sight. While the girls surrounded her, the boys farther away smirked and laughed as Berti explained.

"You can't do that," squealed Gustl.

"I've already done it," cackled Berti. He looked at me, then back at Gustl. "Ask the American. He's already a redskin, and I've just made you an Apache."

"Winnetou," crowed Rupert Bichlhofer, dirtying the name of the great hero from Karl May's adventure books.

Yes, I got to be a brave, but I think only because I'd soon go to America. As a refugee, normally I'd have been a mere cowboy to be sacrificed in an Indian uprising. On our last school days before summer recess all the boys wanted to be Indians. As always Berti played the instigator. He approached me to apply his war paint.

"Shove off," I said, "or I'll poison your well before we go."

He acted hurt. "You may think you're better than us now, going to America and all, but you're still a shit of a neighbor. If it were up to me I'd scalp you personally."

"Get lost. I'm already half the American, and I've learned from Jersey Joe."

"You think you're an artist, don't you? Don't you want to be painted?"

"I've seen enough behinds. More finely drawn than yours."

Gustl Ponkratz, in the meantime, managed to smudge Berti's lipstick war paint all over his pink face, up to his narrow forehead and curly hair. He didn't want anyone to see his face with female parts until he'd fully smudged them. Anyway, the drawings were too awkward for anyone to know. Still, Gustl bounded toward the nearby woods, shamed and petulant. The other boys yelped war cries and chased him uphill.

It looked as if, by smearing his war paint, Gustl had been reduced in rank to a cowboy. Berti, meanwhile, had pulled some chicken feathers from his pocket and stuck them in his hair. As Herbert rolled his eyes, he seemed to be the only chief until Rupert Bichlhofer tore some feathers from his hand.

"Let's get Gustl," Rupert shouted. "He's a paleface!"

Suddenly Gustl turned down toward us from the sloping woods and pulled a pistol from his floppy pants. As Rupert and Berti stopped in awe, Gustl took aim from behind a towering fir. "Pop, pop," his silver pistol exploded. It turned out to be from America, a toy from the American major who'd visited his father on official business.

Flattered by our astonishment, Gustl showed off his weapon, like the time when he paraded his thick bun with meat. Now we could see a red tape with nubs of powder inside the pistol's chamber. Each time Gustl pulled the trigger, the hammer struck the tape and a nub exploded, and each pull fed more buttons forward to be struck.

"Bang, bang," all the boys now shouted, desperate to be equals.

I nudged Herbert. "Curtis Bishop?"

"You may be right—the community liaison. The major seems to be everywhere."

"It's just a damn toy," said Berti, including me in his circle. "Konrad and I find the real thing every day when the Americans maneuver."

"What does that mean?" scoffed Herbert.

"Shells and cartridges," Berti said, "primed and ready."

Herbert looked him up and down. "Like your flapping mouth?"

Berti shut up before the taller Herbert.

"Let's get the cowboys," I said, bored. "Who's a cowboy, anyway?"

"Mostly the girls," said Rupert. "Gustl too, despite his toy."

"The cheese peddler," sniffed Berti.

I felt superior, looking forward to America. Distance vision. It wasn't just the hints of my growth spurt. I wanted that farsighted look of Stefan Marschall and his Mirjam, posed beside their Chevrolet. The afternoon went on for another hour, but the cowboys proved elusive. The girls didn't really want to play, and the rest of us were mostly Indians. That left no one to scalp. Finally Fräulein Seebach called us together and asked me to say something about America and what I felt leaving Austria.

I flushed at all the attention, with everyone expecting me to say something important. Whatever I'd say, I'd probably offend someone. I suppose I wanted to sound interesting. Actually I felt too shy to admit that Fräulein Seebach had been good to me, along with others like Florian Riedl and Frau Hollinger. No matter where or when, the memory of Frau Hollinger's salt-encrusted bread and pretzels would forever cause my knees to weaken. I looked at Herbert Mautner too, and managed to nod.

Suddenly my throat was clenching. I didn't want to hurt Fräulein Seebach's feelings and thought I'd better just shut up. This wasn't what I'd expected. Then it was as though my growth spurt lurched, and I felt dumb and gangly. Sensing my dilemma, Inge Seebach finally said, "You'll learn English in no time, Konrad."

As usual she had perfect timing. "That's what I want to do," I said gratefully.

She smiled. "You've always been quick to pick things up. A little too quick, sometimes," she teased, "but in America that's a virtue."

Berti Krummbacher snickered softly, and Monika Waldegger looked at me as if she might actually miss me. I felt the blood go to my face. I hoped that everyone, especially Monika, thought I was being proud and strong and modest and aware of the importance of the occasion, even if a little tongue-tied.

"You'll let us know, won't you, when you get to Washington?" said Fräulein Seebach. But what made her think of Washington? She produced one of those mysterious paper tissues to dab at her eyes. Once again I realized the idea of such wasteful tissues could only have come from America—in fact from that Curtis Bishop, who parted his odd hair right down the middle and wore that pencil mustache. He seemed to be everywhere and had left Gustl that toy pistol.

Would Inge Seebach be going soon too, I wondered? Maybe joining this Curtis Bishop? My imagination started galloping. Maybe her leaving was inevitable, but somehow it wasn't right. I sneaked a look from side to side but nobody seemed even close to sniffling, unless maybe Monika behind that shy smile. I felt compelled to correct Fräulein Seebach.

"Actually we're going to Chicago, not Washington."

"To join those gangsters, whores, and pimps," I heard a voice say behind me.

I barely heard the words and hoped that no one else could. They came from Berti Krummbacher, snickering in my ear. He knew I couldn't snap back, not with Fräulein Seebach standing before us.

I didn't know how suddenly I found the words. "It's in the heart of the country, along with Kansas," I said, innocent. "There's lots of Germans there, all the way down to Texas."

A faint blush spread toward her forehead. Now I thought I knew. Inge Seebach planned on going too. This Curtis Bishop had persuaded her, this smooth Baptist or Methodist. He didn't deserve her as much as Austria did. Somehow I wanted her to stay in Straubling so I could remember Austria with Fräulein Seebach in it. She didn't belong in Texas, even if things conspired to make it happen.

But maybe I was getting ahead of myself again. I waited for her to speak. I felt numb and blank with disappointment, but grateful too, that at least she'd stayed long enough for me to begin school in Austria. She wasn't Ingrid Klein, the teacher from Romania, who'd deserted her charges even if they included Naz and Poldi, to run off with some Serbian Royalist. Fräulein Seebach's blush subsided.

"Class," she said, recovering, "what do we know about Chicago?"

"Al Capone," volunteered Herbert brutally, as if to test her, "dealt in whiskey, sawed-off shotguns, and massacres. We've all heard about St. Valentine's."

Except for me, I don't think our class knew about the St. Valentine massacre. Herbert just didn't like sentimentality. "That may be one tiny part," our teacher told him calmly. "But no, where is Chicago? Gustl?"

The nervous Gustl scratched his unruly hair. Lantern-faced Norbert Pfeifer would have known the answer, but I assumed he'd finally set foot in Canada. Gustl wasn't stupid, either, but with his mouth always half open, seemed to prefer to drool. I was sure his father, Anton Ponkratz, didn't do so when he flushed his cattle tripe down the creek into the Salzach.

"Anyone?" Fräulein Seebach asked patiently.

"It's in the heart of America, the very heart of it. In the state of Illinois, the Land of Lincoln," dared Monika Waldegger, as though reciting from a geography lesson.

She must have read up on Chicago. I took it as a secret compliment. Her voice was like a bell. Something about it made me think of the little song about Marianne, about how she tugged at heartstrings. My growth spurt wasn't what I had expected.

"It's right by Lake Michigan, just south of Milwaukee. They say the wind's always blowing. It must come off the lake."

"That's excellent, Monika!"

To this day I remember those two voices, Fräulein Seebach's patient lilt and the silver voice of Monika. We stood in a sunny clearing in the tame woods overlooking Straubling. There were no poisonous snakes in all of Austria, but there were snakes in America and especially Texas or Arkansas. Monika's words about Chicago's winds awakened me; I didn't quite know to what.

Although usually the sky was overcast, today not a cloud hovered over Straubling, so far from Jersey Joe's shores. I was still worlds from Chicago and the Wild West and the storm raging in *The Regulators* as the Methodist preacher and his gang plotted for power and gold. But it seemed right that our last day of class came just after Jersey Joe had triumphed over Ezzard Charles.

Once again I imagined Joe's relentless fists. Like pistons fueled by an engine room, they wouldn't stop their hammering. They pounded like our waiting train, beating Charles into history. Jersey Joe was my call to battle—to meet America head-on. My heart was just as big and unruly as an engine room. But as I looked down toward Straubling, I felt loss mixed with romance.

CHAPTER 36

PASSAGE

When the chattering gravel truck pulled up to our hut, Monsignor Bruck's spiritual admonitions still weighed on my mind. Father and I had seen him just after shopping for Mother's cuckoo clock. His counsel wasn't a happy thought, but at least the clock made Mother happy.

"It's a country of great promise," Bruck had told Father. "Of course, the moral dangers are immense." And again, "I'm speaking of temptations, each soul's individual trials. You'll want to look out for Konrad." And still more ominously: "Have you thought of parish schools?"

But on our way toward Salzburg his words finally subsided. As we neared the city, the rain fell as always like a mist over slate roofs and cobbled streets. I saw Father periodically check for me on the truck bed through the cab window, just as I'd crept under a drop cloth from a construction site. Through the last kilometer to the train station the rain fell over the cathedral, over Mozart's misty birthplace on the square, on the Mirabell Gardens, and shrouded the Hohensalzburg fortress on the hill. Near the station and our former camp in Salzburg, as workers cleared out rubble, we passed the broken Hotel Europa.

Florian helped Father slide our trunk off the truck bed as Hias, the waiting driver, stood shifting from one foot to the other. Mother looked ready to cry. They carried the green trunk with New York spelled wrong toward the boarding platform, where the train north to Bremerhaven stood waiting. They heaved it up through a second-class door and tossed our bundles after it.

Suddenly, from the station at the far end, we saw old Resi and Peter Eberhardt hobbling toward us. Father must have told them. Our hometown friends, still waiting in the Salzburg camp, had helped make our departure possible by testifying to my being born. They waited to get to Canada but still hadn't found a sponsor. Years ago a brother of Resi had gone west to Manitoba and glowingly written of wheat fields. They were trying to find his family. Now Resi took Mother's hand.

"Anni, Anni," she repeated, as Mother dabbed at her eyes.

Father hugged old Peter Eberhardt, who as usual didn't say much.

Resi's eyes grew moist. "We couldn't just let you run off, could we? Without someone from back home to see you off?"

"It's wonderful to be able see you," Mother said, looking gratefully at Father.

"We could sponsor you from America," Father suddenly said.

Mother looked surprised, then softened. Resi's smile was blank, as though she hadn't understood. Peter Eberhardt was touched but shook his head.

"That's very generous of you, Hans. It's not that simple; you'll be new arrivals—"

"Maybe I can find an established countryman to do it," Father said. "Unless, of course, you prefer Canada."

On the platform the conductor called on people to board. Our driver almost blubbered when Mother took his hand. The Eberhardts smiled, forlorn. Father patted Florian's shoulder. Suddenly they embraced, tears in their eyes, then Father jumped on the train. Mother and I had already climbed aboard. Goodbyes flew back and forth, and everyone promised to write. I liked them all, but right now I had enough of goodbyes. The conductor whistled, and the train lurched. As it rolled from the station, we waved at Florian from its corridor, and at the driver and the Eberhardts. As it picked up speed they became dots on the boarding platform. Salzburg receded and was gone.

The next day we boarded ship, a troop carrier from the war. After delivering troops to Europe, the empty USS Washburn made return runs back to America. With all the refugees on board, this way they weren't dry runs. The voyage proved to be a grand adventure. The rolling ocean first caught my attention. In the English Channel a breaking storm stacked up the waves. They boiled around the carrier and churned toward the blurred horizon. Between the storm clouds and the sea I glimpsed the tilting cliffs of Dover. Europe fell behind us, receding into darkness.

As the troop carrier tossed, we slept uneasily. We stirred with the other refugees in the same cramped bunks in which the troops going to war in Europe had once slept, only now the ship sailed westward. Not that it seemed to matter. All everyone seemed to do was eat. I think most of us even dreamed of food. I can't say I didn't, but I liked the ocean more.

In the ship's mess you could gorge yourself; no one ever said, "Enough!" This wasn't your camp kitchen or Toni Spitz's black bean soup. People ate as if compelled to eat—consumed breakfast eggs with buttered toast and orange juice, or coffee and toast with marmalade, or finished stews or pot roast, whatever was offered—even if the ship's rolling soon made them give up all they ate. We gathered strength for America, though none of us were real sailors. I wished Herbert Mautner could have seen us; he would have liked the irony.

A second storm surged in the channel even before we reached open ocean. I rode the pitching hull that carved the North Sea like a plow. A faint sound made me turn. There was no one, only the wind across the decks. An old woman struggled past me sucking on a slice of lemon. They said it helped if you got seasick, and especially the adults got sick. When I looked up from the railing, I glimpsed someone on an upper deck. A noise answered from on high, above the thunder of the ship. Someone was throwing up, or rather down. A green veil splotched my shirt as the old woman smirked like Granny Pfeifer.

More refugees wove through the wind, their heads low or sucking on lemons. As soon as the storm cleared, screeching children chased each other. I didn't know anyone aboard since we had held out for America. Vera Kratky wasn't here, or the Hutz girls or little Milan or anyone else from the camp, not even the freckled Norbert. They were bound for Canada, Australia, Baranquilla in Colombia, and who knows where else, but we had held out for America. Yet that night I dreamed of Norbert.

He was off to Moose Jaw, but in my dream I glimpsed him deep within the ship. I didn't like it. And if he was on board, his granny also sailed with us. I turned a corner to elude him, but suddenly saw him stooped beside the Salzach River. "Help me," he groaned. "I can't lift this rock." He had never paid for anything in his life but added, "I'll even give you money."

"Keep it," I said.

"It's just one rock," wheezed Norbert, "but it's covering a jeep axle! It would fetch a good price." His green eyes bulging in his face, he braced his back against a willow and pried his legs against the rock. "Help me," he pleaded. "I can't do it alone."

A rusty troop carrier like the USS Washburn now appeared in the muddy river. I hadn't known the Salzach ran that deep. I suddenly stood high on the carrier's upper deck, watching Norbert strain against his rock. Now Mother approached with Granny Pfeifer. "Help Norbert," she commanded. "You should be ashamed."

But my ship pushed on with Norbert locked in place.

His granny's mouth moved as always. "You'd better find him a doctor," she slavered, "even if he is that Russian. *Eigenlob stinkt!* If he collected scraps like my Norbert—"

So now he was *her* Norbert. For once Mother defended me before even Father could. "What would that prove?"

Still in the dream, I panted in our narrow quarters. Only inches above me swayed another hammock. Someone snored three feet away—a refugee tossed in a dream. Two bunks above me appeared a bushy head. It was the Russian doctor, his accented voice so deep it seemed to echo from a barrel. "You will please now breathe deeply. It will help you to sleep."

"You're here too?" I said, astonished.

"To the victors go the vanquished. This ship sails to America. And now, sweet dreams."

That woke me. Relieved, soon I again enjoyed the voyage. It was the voyage of discovery I'd dreamed of, with Father salting it with dry comments. One day a cook in white apron and two helpers rolled metal trash cans from the kitchen toward the ship's tilting rear. Snowy gulls plunged toward the falling scraps. Dismayed, I saw Father shrug.

"Easy, *strizi*. The ocean's meant to sail on. Can't sail without leaving traces."

For once I liked his word for *rascal*. "They should find another way."

"The fare's more interesting than the bean soup. Good for your growth spurt. But it means scraps get left over."

"What do you mean?"

"Patience," said Father, chuckling, "should we stew in our own juice? We need our strength; we're being fattened up for business as usual in America. We're not refugees now, we're just about Americans!"

He roughed up my hair but I fell stubbornly silent. Aboard ship I'd begun to see him with fresh eyes. It was as though I tried to fly kites, and he kept pulling them down. Yet without him, I couldn't even have dreamed of flying them. But the ocean calmed me—the immensity of the waters as our vessel plowed its way.

I took in images and arranged them in my mind. They startled and delighted me whether the sea was calm or violent. I could have done wonderful ocean scenes in drawing class, surprising Fräulein Seebach. Wedged in my bunk, I even dreamed at night, as we all slept in endless tiers deep within the bowels of the ship. I knew above us soared the night sky as we coursed toward the unknown. We were on our great adventure—our voyage of discovery. And if things ever got too ordinary, Father would shrug, inscrutable as the ocean. One day I saw him from afar during a life jacket drill. In our bloated salmon-colored vests, we all looked puffed up. Yet Father grinned, holding out his ham-sized hands.

"Wouldn't that be something?" giggled a wrinkled refugee who looked like Stipe Baumann. "If we all sank and drowned," he snickered, "on the way to our America?"

Everyone lurched from him, aghast.

"Escape the deluge back there"—and he pointed far beyond the wake—"to drown along the way?"

"For shame!" cried everyone.

Father worked his way toward me through the puffed-up crowd until his padded salmon vest bumped mine. He took the old man in stride. "Just crossing his fingers," he scoffed. "That's all the fellow's doing."

I gulped the salt air, but my voice felt hoarse. "What do you mean?" I said.

"Don't get too serious. Dreams are fine, but never get too comfortable."

We must have looked ludicrous in our vests. "We can't drown anyway, not in these," I said.

"Exactly. And if you fell, I'd yank you up." He said it almost like a dare.

That made me think way back, to the camp when Franjo Boban whacked little Milan. To Father, I guessed, I remained his little shit, but just the same, his pride and joy. For him I was the point of sailing to America. Just then I wondered when I'd tell him about my career plans. I supposed when I was sure. But no matter what they were, I sensed they would disappoint him. I might pick art and drawing, or something just as frivolous and unworthy of our struggle toward America. Engineer or doctor wouldn't do it for me, not even surgeon. I wasn't Herbert.

Whatever it was, it would come easier in America. My job would be to find a way to tell him when the time came, if he didn't know already. But that would be another chapter.

An hour later I saw him swabbing decks with his crew of refugees. As they mopped their way down from the upper tiers, they swore at the coffee and chewed eggs, wrinkled tomato skins, and broth that spattered every deck. A clean carrier was proud and safer as we neared America. Soon, almost imperceptibly, we stood closer to shore. As if entrusted with my delivery, Mother clutched at me. Father's hand was on my shoulder. I let it rest. Gazing toward the bobbing shore, we must have looked like Stefan Marschall and his Mirjam posed beside their dark blue Chevrolet.

I had the mumps as we reached shore. My jaws hurt when I ate oranges, but their flesh tasted sweet. I kept my mouth shut. We could have been quarantined by the port authorities on the emptying ship, within sight of the statue lifting its torch. As we stood waiting, tags with black numbers fluttered on our coats. A hooting tugboat neared yet seemed to stand forever still. I recalled the recent storm that had risen during the night and briefly covered the stars. It was like one last upheaval that scooped us up and spat us on land.

Just then, right off America, I didn't even think of Jersey Joe.

ABOUT THE AUTHOR

The author escaped Communist Eastern Europe after World War II, discovered a love of drawing as a schoolboy in Austria, and a passion for writing when he eventually reached America. They helped him balance teaching English and twenty years as an American diplomat working in Africa, Europe, and South America. He studied English and writing at the University of California, Berkeley, and the University of Oregon, and has published fiction and poetry in literary magazines. ***Discovering America*** is his first published novel.

ABOUT THE BOOK

Konrad Kemper, the young hero of ***Discovering America,*** dreams irrepressibly of America in a refugee camp in postwar Austria. In the process he discovers not only his own quirky America, but encounters a stew of survivors scrambling to move on from the rubble of the war—refugees from Eastern Europe, Austrian townsfolk, and even American soldiers. Konrad's hard-bitten story combines grit and a comic edge, and finally hope and growing up.

Printed in the United States
By Bookmasters